YES, COMRADE!

EMERGENT LITERATURES

Emergent Literatures is a series of international scope that makes available, in English, works of fiction that have been ignored or excluded because of their difference from established models of literature.

MANUEL RUI

YES, COMRADE!

★

Foreword by **Gitahi Gititi**

Translated by **Ronald W. Sousa**

 University of Minnesota Press
Minneapolis
London

Copyright 1993 by the Regents of the University of Minnesota

Originally published as *Sim Camarada!* © Angolan Writers' Union, 1977, Lisbon.

Emanuel Corgo, "Against Negritude," Manuel Rui, "New Sea," reprinted from *Poems from Angola*, trans. Michael Wolfers (London: Heinemann, 1979), by permission of Michael Wolfers.

Published by the University of Minnesota Press
2037 University Avenue Southeast, Minneapolis, MN 55455-3092
Printed in the United States of America on acid-free paper

Library of Congress Cataloging-in-Publication Data

Rui, Manuel.
    [Sim camarada! English]
    Yes, comrade! / Manuel Rui ; translated by Ronald W. Sousa ; foreword by Gitahi Gititi.
       p.   cm. — (Emergent literatures)
    ISBN 0-8166-1966-2 (alk. paper)
    I. Title. II. Series.
PQ9929.R8S5613 1993
869.3 — dc20   92-32341
                                           CIP

Jacket design by Jeanne Lee
Book design by Patricia M. Boman

. . . and along all the roads of tears flowers raged,
saying, with a smile: "Yes, comrade!"

Contents

Foreword

Gitahi Gititi

Manuel Rui was born in 1941 in Huambo, Angola. In 1961 he went to the University of Coimbra in Portugal, where he obtained his law degree in 1969; thereafter he practiced law in Coimbra and Viseu. His legal practice involved providing advice to various trade unions. In addition, Rui was on the editorial boards of several literary journals, including *Vértice*. This involvement led to his arrest in 1973 on charges of political activity for the MPLA (Popular Movement for the Liberation of Angola). He returned to Angola in 1974 after the overthrow of the fascist regime in Portugal; he served as a director-general of information at the request of the postcoup Portuguese authorities. It was also in 1974 that FAPLA (the People's Armed Forces for the Liberation of Angola) was formally launched as a guerrilla force. In January 1975, upon nomination by the MPLA, Rui was appointed minister of information in the transitional government comprising the MPLA, the FNLA, and UNITA (National Union for the Total Independence of Angola) in the period just before independence. It is from such a vantage point that Manuel Rui gives us a literary rendering of the problems inherent in the formative days of the fledgling nation.

After independence, Rui was appointed head of the MPLA's Department for External Relations and in May 1976 was nominated as people's prosecutor in the People's Revolutionary Tribunal; in June 1976, the latter tried and convicted British and U. S. prisoners for mercenary activity in Angola during 1975 and 1976. For most of 1977, Manuel Rui was director of the MPLA's new Department of Revolutionary Orientation, formed after the dissolution of the Ministry of Information.

The fiercely optimistic note in *Yes, Comrade!* is built on the apparently anonymous, but highly allegorical, epigraph:

> . . . *and along all the roads of tears flowers raged,*
> *saying, with a smile: "Yes, comrade!"*

The verb *zangar*, which Ronald Sousa translates as "to rage," suggests the passion that moves patriotic Angolans to rid their country of all vestiges of colonialism as well as certain traces of precolonial traditions that bar the way to the achievement of a higher plane of human existence. Manuel Rui etches this process as a difficult, but not impossible, road, a protracted revolutionary struggle whose sacrifices yield the flowers that spring forth, defying death and smilingly daring to say Yes! to life. This unyielding resolve to overcome the atrocities of the past and the imperfections of the present is shared by many Angolan writers, especially those who rallied around the MPLA and its revolutionary vision for Angola:

> *The whip scored our naked backs*
> *in the coal mines*
> *in the cane plantations*

or when we said NO

but we are not prisoners of history

. . . .

Today the people demand that we fight

with weapons in hand

and that we struggle

and that we struggle

once twice or a thousand times

until there is built a better world.

Emanuel Corgo, "Against Negritude"

I

It should be noted that the analysis of cultural reality already gives a measure of the strengths and weaknesses of the people when confronted with the demands of the struggle, and therefore represents a valuable contribution to the strategy and tactics to be followed, on the political as well as the military plane.

Amilcar Cabral

The place of culture in the struggle for total decolonization has been widely recognized in African political thought, especially in the postindependence epoch when debate has raged over the form and content of education; the use of indigenous languages; the identification and definition of national culture; and the (re)writing of history. Continental and national manifestos attest to the paramountcy of culture, as do the writings of Amilcar Cabral, Samir Amin, Eduardo Mondlane, Julius Nyerere, Kwame Nkrumah, Frantz Fanon, Ngugi wa Thiong'o, and Albert Memmi, to name but a few.

Given the suppression of African cultural production under European colonialism, there is general consensus that the achievement of the political kingdom must accompany and sometimes supersede the abstract theorization of questions pertaining to culture. Issues of literary theory and the creation and extension of a national literature seem to be inseparable from the struggle to banish those conditions that dehumanize people and render impossible the unfettered growth and vitality of cultural production consonant with economic and political freedom. And especially for an intellectual elite nursed at the colonial teat, the task is one of recuperating certain cultural roots and imaginatively articulating them to a productive present-day economy. An incisive model for this process was proposed by Guinea (Bissau)'s Amilcar Cabral, who envisaged a "return to the roots":

In the framework of the conquest of national independence and in the perspective of developing the economic and social progress of the people, the objectives must be at least the following: development of a popular culture and all positive indigenous cultural values;

development of a national culture
based upon the history and the
achievements of the struggle itself . . .
as well as patriotism, of the spirit of
sacrifice and devotion to the cause of
independence, of justice and of
progress . . . of a universal culture for
perfect integration into the
contemporary world . . . of solidarity,
of respect and disinterested devotion
to human beings.

II

The "stories" that constitute *Sim Camarada!* mark a significant moment in both the literary and the political history of Angola, pertaining as they do to the moment just before and immediately after independence and the enormous task of national (re)constitution and refiguration. The lead story is precisely about how to go about constructing a model for the necessary weaving and reweaving of the narrative of the nation and its constituent parts. But building a "nation" in Africa often means erecting a new and tension-ridden political amalgam on the ground razed by European colonialism. The "nation" that the departing colonial power had arbitrarily "established" had never had an authentic dialogue with itself, had never convened all its constituencies to determine membership, house rules, the running and accounting of its business, until the breathtaking moment of a euphoric, but demanding, *independencia.* How was a nascent Angola going to establish an order that neutralized the chaos and violence of Portugal's last desperate stand? More specifically, how was the MPLA government, having taken the popular mandate upon independence in 1975, going to deal with the deadly, destructive rivalry of a Zaire-supported FNLA and a South Africa-bankrolled UNITA? The MPLA leadership had to find urgent solutions to unemployment, grinding poverty, the resettlement of the war-displaced and orphans, the (mainly political) reeducation of almost the entire Angolan population, and the elimination of crime, corruption, and illgotten privilege. "Five Days after Independence" presents a staggering picture of the capital, Luanda, and an embattled MPLA in deadly combat against remnant Portuguese troops in alliance with other "freedom fighters."

The first story, "The Council," exposes the ineptitude and self-serving nature of the Junta Governative Portuguesa. In clearly satirical terms, Manuel Rui portrays the junta as "an international government. It had constituent parties. The Angolan party, the Portuguese party, the American, the French, the Zairians, the German, and the et cetera parties. But as the Portuguese party came barely holding its pants up because of Spinolar indigestion, that is, as the imperial party controlled the Portuguese party, we can speak of only two parties: the Angolan and the imperial." The "council" in question quite literally demonstrates the diverse contesting powers and political interest represented in the postindependence "coalition." It also symbolically foregrounds future debates on the important question of who and what are more authentically Angolan, measured in terms of a commitment to an Angolan cultural and political autonomy.

Although it is common to associate literature or narrative with the printed word, and especially that which is available in European languages, it should be remembered that a comparatively vaster body of the narrative of Angolan history—precolonial, colonial, and postindependence—still resides in the oral tradition. In a significant number of cases, even what is written remains unpublished. Many Angolan writers now recognize and use the creative possibilities contained in orature with its nonfixed and open-ended format. Both "The Watch" and "Five Days after Independence" move forward on a momentum provided by the framework of orature. The story-within-a-story rubric, a particular feature of the "oral" tradition, is indeed the very dynamic that propels the history of Angola, in particular the "new" stories that must be recounted in the form of a collective countermemory and as oppositional cultural practice. Orature has perforce become an indispensable component of contemporary Angolan narrative. The term *estória,* first used by José Luandino Vieira to designate the open-ended and multilayered narratives he started writing in the early 1960s under the influence of orature, has now become a common feature in the writings of other Angolan writers, including Manuel Rui.

What are the objective conditions under which the production and distribution of literature are possible? What are the ideological and discursive spaces within which the builders of a nation hope to endow it with a worthy cultural product? It is interesting to note that the original Portuguese edition of *Yes, Comrade!* was published in not Angola but in Portugal by Ediçoes 70 for the Union of Angolan Writers because at the time all operative printing presses in Angola were being mobilized in the revolutionary effort. Manuel Rui's manuscript was printed in Lisbon and then returned to Angola, paralleling in the process the route taken by the timepiece in "The Watch," manufactured in Europe (with materials readily available in Angola) and then imported as a finished product. How will a future Angola avoid the pitfalls of dependency? As for literature, will its creation continue to reproduce calcified narrative strategies based on the authority of omniscient "elders," or will it dare to be young, adventurous, and open-minded? "The Watch" is the story of a watch; it is also the story of the telling of the story of a watch. The commander views the telling of the story as a project that allows him to construct himself in tomorrow: "It was a treat for him to be in the midst of that group of children who were so quick and forced him to embellish the story of the watch with such details as had never before even passed through his head." Through a gesture reminiscent of the link "between the sea foam and waves under the open blue of the sky," the unfinished is manifested as a model for the depiction of reality, "because what was really real was the story being told."

Not many writers are able to register the anticipation, the thrill, the pathos, the ambivalent newness of the very idea of "We're free now!" as ably and sensitively as Manuel Rui does in "Two Queens of Carnival." In the abstract, the idea of laying down one's life for the people is an attractive one. But what is a mother to feel when, caught up in the emotion of celebrating the still-warm victory, news reaches her that her son is in the mortuary, dead? "Two Queens" dramatizes such a mother's agonizing but ready recognition that in the common struggle an apotheosis is possible only with the acceptance of the sure possibility of death in the execution of a chosen and sacred duty.

The revolutionary ethos that permeates much of Angolan writing, especially in the years immediately preceding independence and afterward, signals its consciousness of intertextuality. Hence the almost automatic domestication of the Portuguese language, the signaling of the daily coexistence and interaction of Portuguese with indigenous Angolan languages—often, indeed, the displacement or devaluation of Portuguese words, phrases, and concepts by items from other Angolan languages. Hence the widespread sharing of symbolism, event, and emphasis. The arduous task of nation building—the resolution and clarification of ideological antagonisms; the forging of a revolutionary ideal devoid of racist, ethnic, or sexist chauvinisms; the articulation of a corpus of enduring cultural models and a projection of a viable economic-political polity—is the primary theme that brings together the works of Manuel Rui, Uanhenga Xitu, Pepetela, José Luandino Vieira, and others.

The sea (water) as the ultimate symbol of growth, regeneration, and hope recurs throughout Rui's writing, as it does in Pepetela's (Artur Carlos Mauricio Pestana dos Santos's) *Mayombe* and in José Luandino Vieira's *The Real Life of Domingos Xavier*. It is already manifest, for example, in Manuel Rui's poem "Mar novo" ("New Sea"), in which both economic and cultural production, articulated to solidarity and egalitarianism, have the capacity to restore us to a more humane, "newborn" world:

And it is good to examine hands. Especially

our hands moistened by the sea.

Hands that touch things.

Hands that do things.

Hands. Hands as terminal for the loading

and unloading of our thought.

Hands submerged under water

in timid (re)discovery of the essential

in submarine pulse of a new hope.

This vision of the sea as a trope for unbounded possibility is already signaled in Manuel Rui's second collection of poems *A Onda* (The wave), first published in 1973; it is further enhanced in "The Watch" where, at the very end, the coweavers of the narrative of national reconstruction ("that story that sailed from mouth to mouth among the children like a musical boat on an infinite rainbow sea"), the Commander and the children, round off their Sunday storytelling by "rejoining" their source of inspiration:

> *Joyfully laughing and jumping, one*
> *by one the children ran to the water*
> *and dived in,* each in his or her
> special way.
> *The ocean was serene as always,*
> *there on that beach that extended a*
> *long way out. A children's beach.*
> *Blue transparent sea revealing a*
> *bottom with shells and conches*
> *beyond imagination. [The*
> *Commander] . . . stayed [on the*
> *water's edge]* in a draft of dreams
> and hope, taking in the sea and the
> horizon as if they were the beginning
> and end of the same story.
> *(Emphasis added.)*

The "children" whom Manuel Rui eulogizes in "Five

Days after Independence" have already played and will continue to play an unprecedented political and social role in Angola. It is unthinkable that they can go back to being children or that they will not wrest certain roles and prerogatives from the erstwhile holders of such offices, just as they effectively change the course of the story of the watch in response to dialectical necessity. As a representative group that has participated in the liberation struggle, they must participate in the forging of a national identity. The telling of the story of the watch has opened the door to a new collective cultural tradition consonant with the logic of a revolutionary enterprise:

> *Comrade Commander and the*
> *children were rewriting, repaginating,*
> *with enthrallment growing to*
> *crescendos, were bringing to an end*
> *that never ended, that story more of*
> *love and hope than of hate and war*
> *that no writer would ever know how*
> *to put down on paper.*

Thousands of young boys and girls, of different ethnic backgrounds, died anonymously in combat or were the hapless victims of the torture and carnage unleashed by Portuguese troops in their last-ditch desperation to curtail the armed resistance. Others died at the hands of the FNLA and UNITA, the two other movements opposed to the ascendancy of the MPLA. These were the *pioneiros;* the armed struggle leading to Angola's liberation can hardly be told without paying them homage. The *pioneiros* are the collective hero of "Five Days after Independence," but already their story appears in "The Watch": it is the *pioneiros* who retrieve the watch from a Zairian mercenary who enters Luanda as part of the FNLA push for control of the capital in the last days of the liberation struggle. The link between the juvenile *pioneiros* as *possibilitadores* for the recapture of the watch and the youngsters who wrest the "traditional" ending of the story from the retired commander is immediately obvious: the *pioneiros* and the commander's auditors are twin sets of the dialectic of transformation through struggle, diversification, and invention. As Manuel Rui himself signals in "New Sea," "Nothing endures except / for the necessary change."

It is significant that Rui dedicates his *11 Poemas en novembro (ano dois)* (Eleven poems in November [year 2]) (1977) to "the *pioneiros* of my country." November 11, 1975, is, of course, the national anniversary of Angolan independence. The revolutionary and heroic role of the *pioneiros* has also been celebrated in poems such as Fernando Costa Andrade's "Ernesto Ngangula" (1969). Ernesto Ngangula was a twelve-year-old boy who was beaten to death by Portuguese soldiers because he would not reveal the location of his people-run school and an MPLA detachment. This was on December 1, 1968, now celebrated as Pioneers' Day. April 14, 1968, commemorates Youth Day; it is the date when the *pioneiro* José Mendes de Carvalho, or "Hoji Ya Henda," was cut down in an assault on a Portuguese military post in eastern Angola. "Hoji Ya Henda" is immortalized in such poems as Jofre Rocha's "Last Talk with Zeca Mendes" (1968) and Rui de Matos's "I'm Looking for a Lion." In "Five Days after Independence," Manuel Rui emphasizes that the new writing that is "under way [here in Angola]" must record the valiant deeds of all who sacrificed their lives for a liberated Angola "so that there

can be told all the stories of all the youngsters who are forever going to walk tossed on the foam of that blue sea of
ours." The young woman Carlotta, who evolves into a
symbolic sister-mother-wife of the *pioneiros,* gains the impression that "the lights, the walls, held within them a multitude of stories to be told, of numbers of people assassinated, stories of the anonymous popular resistance." The
format of the "estória," evident in the recurrent, formulaic
"There were four of them in two ranks . . . ," is Manuel
Rui's tribute to the indissoluble relationship between the
role the *pioneiros* have discharged and the culture of a future Angola that will forever bear the marks of a past renewed through revolutionary struggle.

A revolution, it could be said, is also a sanitary and
socially rehabilitative exercise that clears away such colonial poisons as prostitution and self-abasement. How to
overcome relativistic prejudices against "prostitutes"?
How to eliminate social chauvinism and readmit "undesir-
ables" into Angolan society? The narrative of "The Last
Bordello" reveals the real enemy to be the bloodthirsty
Zaire-supported mercenaries of the FNLA, not the "prostitutes" at the bordello, who already manifest a humanness
and compassion impossible in the mercenaries. As Mana
Domingas and the women of the former bordello, having
shed the trappings of their erstwhile "trade," join other *ca-
maradas* on the streets of Luanda, "the night [is] enveloped
by the usual freshness of the sea breeze, and, in the sky,
some stars [shine], while the silence [seems] to promise a hiatus in these disastrous times." Manuel Rui thus
poses the question of the rehabilitation of the *lumpenpro-
letariat.*

Ronald Sousa's excellent translation of *Sim Camarada!* now makes available for readers of English one of the
most riveting and challenging literary works to come out
of Angola. *Yes, Comrade!* is unparalleled both in Angolan

and African literature as a sensitive, searching portrayal of that gripping moment when the celebration of victory is still colored by the smoke and dust raised by the departing enemy. Still, that victory is certain!

Translator's Preface

It is put forth as a sort of truism that translation is an "impossibility." If "impossibility" admits of degree, then what follows is more "impossible" than most exercises in translation. As a consequence, I feel it necessary to advise the reader about the ensuing pages and the relationship they bear to an original called *Sim Camarada!*

The five stories that constitute this volume are set in July and August 1975, the period of civil war in Luanda, the capital city of Angola, and in the immediately following months, ending with the proclamation, in November of that year, of the People's Republic of Angola. Those events end a period set in motion in April of 1974 with the collapse of Portuguese colonialism. The stories are written from within the discourse of the MPLA (Popular Movement for the Liberation of Angola), the victor in the Luanda civil war and the eventual basis for the government of the People's Republic.

The stories, with to some extent the exception of "The Watch," have as their implicit readership people with some knowledge of the war of independence and especially of the civil war in the capital city. References to urban geography abound, as do allusions to specific individuals, events, groups, organizations, and discourse phenomena of the time. Those allusions come in a language that relies to a considerable extent both on local Portuguese and on African-language lexical items, usually from the Kimbundu tongue, which predominated in Luanda. Furthermore, some of the local Portuguese terms have meaning only within the context of the civil war and the clash of ideologies that it articulated.

Such factors as these put a severe strain on the possibilities of translation. The original is quite informal, at times seemingly the transcription of speech, with definite rhythms and sound plays; it invites reading aloud. With those same gestures, however, it also explores the discourses that locate individuals and groups in political terms. Thus there is, theoretically speaking, the need for the translator to reproduce diction, rhythm, tone, and other language particularities, to make clear the political attributions encoded in the language as well as the references to place and event, and to have the stories make sense to an English-speaking reader. I have found it impossible to do all of those things in one rendition.

My choices have been as follows. I try to concentrate on certain aspects of the language of the original and on the basics of each story's plot. In the former area, I focus on re-creation of an informal tone, distinctive rhythms (though ones by no means directly imitative of what is found in the original), and general diction. I have chosen not to "inform" the reader of what is meant by many of the allusions; that is, I seldom extend the text to include implicit "explanation." Such explanation as I feel necessary for basic understanding (i.e., explanation of key issues or of important matters that context will not make reasonably clear) is given in brief footnotes and in the List of Organizations. Much that is not vital is left unexplained, since I take my goal to be translation of a specific language performance, not the production of a book of cultural history.

Such tactics, while representing a resolution of sorts in many problem areas, nonetheless leave many questions aside. Much of the stories' diction is quite problematic in itself. For example, one sees virtually throughout the volume the depiction of a struggle between the discourses of cultural nationalism, profiled especially in the language attributed to the FNLA (National Front for the Liberation of Angola) characters, and the Marxist-Leninist discourses of the MPLA. Indeed, "The Last Bordello" can be said to revolve around that issue, telescoped in the struggle between the cultural-nationalist terms *sister* and *brother* (the latter often, because of the FNLA's Zairian connections, rendered as "*frère*") and the MPLA's leveling term *comrade*, which also gives the volume's title its peculiar resonance.

Even more complex are the problems presented by the labels for the various groups and movements. Most of them are given in abbreviations such as I use here, which are then themselves often apocopated or otherwise adapted to specific contexts, quite often in relation to the (implicitly oral) phraseology within which they occur. Sometimes they are to be (sub)vocalized as a sequence of names for letters of the alphabet (that is, they are to be "spelled out"), while at other times the letter sequences are to be treated as acronyms. There are also hybrids between those two poles. In effect, then, each term comes with its own rules and possibilities. A term such as MPLA, for example, is rendered in several different ways in the original. Moreover, the original is itself inconsistent about how some of those labels are represented typographically. Having no handy resources upon which to draw to render that variety in English, I have homogenized all such terms into uniform labels composed of letter sequences. That practice can claim the values of clarity and consistency but also the drawback of an inevitable reduction of linguistic variety—and it has no value at all as far as the implicit orality of the original text is concerned.

As regards the specific local terms, most of them have proved difficult to translate into English in a way that maintains their distinctiveness and, conversely, have been awkward to keep in their original form within an English text. Most therefore have simply disappeared in the translation process, quite often either paraphrased or made into standard English terms. A small number, most of them originally Kimbundu lexical items, remain because they seem to me to be clear and effective in the contexts in which they occur in the English. I readily admit that I would be hard pressed to produce criteria in justification of the tactic adopted in any given instance, save to say that to my mind the choices made further the goals I have with regard to the language tone and texture I wish to create.

Finally, I have been unable to capture much of what I see as the author's gentle ironizing of many of these language phenomena themselves.

It is my hope that, within the manifest "impossibility" of anything like a total "translation," what has emerged from this concentration on select areas of an extremely complex set of originals will still provide rewarding reading.

In the preparation of this translation I have received invaluable aid from Phyllis Reisman Butler, especially in work on "The Watch." And I would like to thank Russell Hamilton, both for the sharing of his knowledge of the history of the time, place, and language involved and his insights into the stories themselves and for his painstaking work on the draft manuscript. While I share any successes with these colleagues, all but needless to say, the final choices in translating—and therefore the final burden of any failure of those choices—rest with myself.

YES, COMRADE!

The Council

Things were just as bad as ever out there. Worse, actually, since now the people were forever staring toward the Government Palace in great consternation. For on this first day of the so-called Angolan government, greater than any other government in the world because it had, count'em, no fewer than three prime ministers, one of those three new ministers came out on the balcony and droned on about how the Palace now belonged to the people. And what is more, he went on to say that the Palace that before had been held by the colonizers had now passed into the hands of its legitimate owners. And the people applauded the minister's words, their eyes wide with independence, arms waving in the air in such a way as to make some dare think that the pages of history had in fact been turned. All that had been necessary was to lick your fingertip, place it on the page, and flip it over!

"Man! This government just can't get it together. See what I mean? Our comrades in people-power clothes and the others, some dressed like Mobutu,* the rest in coats

---

* Mobutu Sese Seko, born Joseph Mobutu, president of Zaire, the country bordering Angola on the north.

and ties. I mean if that's any indication of the differences, this government's going nowhere. I'd throw the whole lot out right now!" one comrade pontificated aloud to himself as he leaned against a tree.

To which another man, recently arrived from Lisbon, seized the opportunity to add: "What is needed is for the contradictions to be laid bare and for the peasant-proletariat coalition to take the Palace by storm as soon as possible so that we can make that qualitative leap forward."

"Oh, come on! 'Leap forward' and all that? Comrade, you must have swallowed a dictionary. Either you're an intellectual or you inherited a library. Get a grip on things!"

But the other man was already disappearing into the crowd.

January thirty-first came and went. And the heat went indifferently on, searing the faces of the stevedores, of the factory workers, all still laboring at the same old wages or, when the wages did go up, still not being able to keep up with the corresponding rise in prices.

It was then that strikes broke out in active response to the new Palace, which, the people well knew, was being run by dedicated people, but in the main they were reactionaries busy putting together an orchestra whose assistant conductor was one Silva Cardoso (may he rest in peace!).

And from the Palace came voices counseling suspension of the strikes in the name of the national economy.

Then came students, to lambast one minister whose habit it was to speak little. As a matter of fact, that made him seem about normal, so, to be more precise, he had the habit—or mania—of being normal. Everything "would be clear later." Therefore, this high-and-mighty pighead of a minister would set forth in public proclamation what was already obvious in practice: that quartz was so resistant to both inductive and deductive reasoning that it moved a silent and bloody war against all who ate bread and butter for breakfast. But of course he himself consumed ten loaves every morning, along with five kilos of ham and six cheeses brought in from Huambo—tribalism completely aside, of course.

What with the workers caught in this ebb and flow, the students competing for the Nobel Prize in stupidity, and the FNLA forces seeking support from the aforementioned Silva Cardoso forces, who had gone so far as to shoot in the air when confronted by some high-school kids, transition was moving ahead full sail in search of its destiny—which, if justice were to be served, would have been for everyone to get the destiny that he or she deserved. Transition was moving ahead full sail by issuing decrees read by no one.

On the asphalt, Luanda was mobbed like never before with foreign tourists! Their customary arrival, camera slung over a shoulder, press card, and air of knowing things, inventing whatever else they might need, eating shrimp and lobster at Pim's or at the Barracuda, huge conto-plus* meals topped off with cigars.

And ever the aforementioned heat. Ever sweat, just like in the old days.

Even so, Savimbi† promised everything but air conditioning for the streets, free deodorant, and a press that turned out thousand-escudo notes under a patent registered in the name "Chipenda Haven."‡

---

* A conto is a thousand-escudo note, the largest bank note in circulation.
† Jonas Savimbi, leader of the UNITA forces.
‡ Daniel Chipenda broke with the MPLA and took with him a substantial number of troops. During the civil war some of his troops, under commanders known as "Chipendas," sided with the FNLA, a few with UNITA, and a considerable number with the MPLA. Within MPLA discourse, the term *Chipenda* is often little more than a synonym for "imperialist."

He had a magic walking stick. You readers will have to forgive me, but, you know, Angolans really are lacking in respect! Consider this: Valentim* also had one of those miraculous walking sticks. And wouldn't you know that the first time UNITA took a beating down south one of our comrades got hold of that walking stick. Now he uses it here in Luanda against those alley cats he calls leftist.† That's one to think about!

The excessive air conditioning, consonant with the long European carpet, the candelabra, the huge table, and the Louis I-don't-know-how-many chairs tilted reality toward somewhat distant latitudes. Here in this salon of the select there were even crystal glasses serving water and well-chilled passion fruit juice. And coffee in good porcelain from the times of the caravels. And there was a waiter dressed in white with gold buttons. And sometimes he wore white gloves too!

A time of grand neologisms enriching the national lexicon much beyond anything "Lusotropicalism" ever portended. Their "Excellencies," the even more than revered ministers from Zaire, Switzerland, or Germany, enjoyed great "augmentatations" made possible by "afluctations" in the authentically imported legislative "precedures," all the while feeling "catastrophied" whenever the matter of "power to the people" came up. They had—surrealistically—put a diamond in a water buffalo's belly, or maybe in a bee swarm, and then everyone was left to strike a deal with the precious stone he or she found, long live prospecting! Or at least that was the position defended by one archaeological personage who, because of the throw of the

---

* Valentim was a follower of Savimbi.
† *Leftist* is a negative term in this context.

dice at the Alvor treaty agreement,* had ended up a public health minister, complete with an old suit lent him by his uncle. The one with the jaguar cap!

At this very moment a tardy "Excellence" made his appearance, tardy not only mentally, you understand, but chronologically as well. The unfortunate Tavares! His head bespeaking the shrewdness of a burglar giving his victim a hornet sting. His jowls quivering with the fullness of the many transitional thousand-escudo notes, not to mention sinister smugglings of French wine and other such stuff. But, with an imbecility beyond even that of the high Portuguese official who, in times gone by, sent a warship to Bailundo, His Excellence regularly gave out his views to the press, braying about matters of domestic and foreign trade. His lips swollen with drafts of cynicism. In his eyes, along with the reflected cerebral myopia, the hint of a self-imposed conviction that he represented genius merely awaiting its revelation. In his hand, the ministerial portfolio. He was what you might call a minister with portfolio!

When it came time to decide about the decree under debate at His Excellence's arrival, he stared hard at his copy of the predistributed document, whispering through the text with his lips.

After various orators had requested permission and spoken in favor of the proposed measures, among them the luminaries in the Tavares line, His Excellence requested a turn as well: "As regards the first article, I stand opposed. Nevertheless the second article, also opposed, OK? I vote against the third, OK? And I want it made clear that as for

---

* A reference to the January 1975 meeting in Alvor, Portugal, of representatives of the FNLA, the MPLA, and UNITA to set up a process and timetable for Angolan independence. They set November 11, 1975, as the date of independence and reached an accord whereby until that date power would lie in the hands of a transitional government.

the fourth I am also opposed. I reject the fifth. OK? The sixth, likewise."

And in this wisest of all orations, the super-superior Tavares went right on rejecting everything until he got to the last article; the High Commissioner was by now in a sound sleep, dreaming of bringing Cabinda by ship to a village in the Portuguese Minho—after the transition, of course.

" . . . I agree with article fifty-six. I do not, however, understand why it is 'article fifty-six' when it could simply be 'article the last.' "

The article read as follows: "This decree shall be effective immediately."

Even the High Commissioner, in his great disillusionment after having until recently been a partner with some Americans in an oil-well venture, was by now lost in thought, his brow furrowed.

"Pardon me. But if you vote against everything in the text, why do you accept the last article, which is nothing more than a formality, a practical measure, an instrument?" asked one of the ministers from the Portuguese contingent. (The uninitiated reader should be aware that this was an international government. It had constituent parties. The Angolan party, the Portuguese party, the American, the French, the Zairian, the German, and the et cetera parties. But as the Portuguese party came barely holding its pants up because of Spinolar* indigestion, that is, as the imperial party controlled the Portuguese party, we can speak of only two parties: the Angolan and the imperial.)

---

* An allusion to General António Spínola, in whose name the 1974 Portuguese revolution was fought.

Tavares, without even focusing his eyes, rejoined: "But then it goes into effect immediately, doesn't it?"

"Yes," said the Portuguese minister.

"Then I agree. Because it goes into effect immediately. OK?"

"Then what are your misgivings?" a confused Angolan minister intervened.

"*Mon frère,* it's because I thought it would go into effect immediately."

"But then you are in agreement?" asked the Portuguese minister again as the Angolans laughed and passed notes back and forth.

"I am and I am not. To be or not to be, that is the question of 'precedure.' That is why it should not go into effect immediately, isn't it?"

"While I am not supposed to take part in the debates, I think that the Commerce Secretary has made a very positive and important contribution," said the High Commissioner, putting his hand to his forehead at the sheer force of that conclusion.

"Thank you muchly," the unfortunate Tavares replied.

"That being so," the presiding figure elucidated, "Brother Tavares is in agreement."

"Obviously," that tribune then affirmed, with a victorious smile.

"If no one has anything more to 'adjute,' according to the agenda we are en route to the next item. Brother Tavares has the floor."

"Yes, Brother Prime Minister, I shall proceed with my own proposal. OK?"

Outside, at the port, the stevedores announced that the strike would go on. Groups of onlookers continued to congregate in front of the Palace to watch the Mercedes and the Peugeots come and go.

Suddenly, His Excellence's briefcase flew open on its own, popping its clasps with a loud noise, and from the case there began to emerge a diarrhea of cigars, many falling on the table, hitting some Excellences in the head, cluttering the carpet.

At which point some Excellences threw themselves avidly upon the cigars, filled their pockets, put three or four in their mouths at once, lit up, exhaled the smoke, and faces began growing indistinguishable in the penumbra.

At this juncture, His Presiding Excellence proclaimed: "It seems to me that Brother Tavares's proposal is approved by acclamation."

"By whose acclamation? C'mon, let's at least vote," one of the Angolans argued in return.

"What? 'Augmentatations' of 'people power' again? I think we ought to suspend the session for coffee."

The waiter with the gold buttons appeared, accompanied by the tinkling of porcelain and crystal.

Outside, a man of the people who had been seated on those benches of desperation in front of the Palace watched some boys pass by dressed in camouflage, looked out on the distant sea, stretched, and then walked away with his hands in his pockets. Empty pockets.

Queried by a friend who asked him what he had been so involved in, the man replied: "Transition!"

The Watch

"Comrade Commander! Tell the story again."

Now and again on Sundays, here in that house right near the ocean, the commander would enjoy the short, deserved repose of the warrior.

The children would begin to arrive in the hope of hearing the story about the watch. The ones who lived on the beach knew the story by heart, and each one, with his or her own flair, would tell it over again here under the shade of the coconut palms, each time with new marvel, a growing to crescendo of inventing that story that sailed from mouth to mouth among the children like a musical boat on an infinite rainbow sea.

All the children from that place knew the story of the watch, and they would retell it at every opportunity. But the real pleasure was to hear it on Sundays, when they were curled up in the sand or in the shade of the small veranda. To receive it meticulous and sweet straight from Comrade Commander's mouth. For he spoke very slowly, at times savoring a cherished detail with his eyes gazing far out on that endless ocean or chewing over a pause inspired deep in the hot sea smell overflowing in the air.

By the time the commander came to the doorway the veranda would be overflowing. Some children playing games with stones and shells, others dripping water from their last dive into the ocean, still others holding half-opened coconuts, but all of them ready to listen to the words of Comrade Commander.

He would slowly sit himself down and put his crutches together on the ground. He would ease his upper body into the chair back, unbutton his shirt, and lean back in deep contemplation before starting in on the story. The children sat transfixed, with beauty in their eyes and hunger in their ears, in silent attention.

The commander always began the same way: "The watch was manufactured in Switzerland, and the brand was Omega."

"And where is Switzerland?"

"Very far away. It's not a person. It's a country, very far, in Europe, where it's very cold."

Such was the custom. The children always interrupted. They shot out new questions, and every time the commander told the story there was something added to it, not only because he had to call up parts from his imagination in response to the children's curiosity but also because they, too, participated in re-creating the narrative, from time to time giving a new twist to the plot.

"Comrade Commander, have you ever been to this Switzerland?"

"Just to pass through."

"And so? The watch?"

"Oh, yes. It was made in Switzerland. There, children like you help to put together, take apart, and repair watches."

The children's mouths would drop open! How wonderful it would be to help put together and take apart watches!

The waves sang softly as they came and went, rolling lightly over the sand and pebbles on the beach. At that hour, on Sunday. Women busy preparing lunch, the good smells in the air of sardines grilling, beans with palm oil, and other delicacies. Pigs, ducks, and chickens roaming about, with no pens or coops. And here, in that small yellow house with the red doors at the edge of the sea, where two posters testified to the fact that Valodia and Gika* had once stayed there, Comrade Commander continued: "One day, up there in Portugal, the watch was sold, along with a lot of other watches."

"And who sold the watch in Portugal?"

"The owner of the factory, who was named Fritz. From Switzerland."

Comrade Commander lit a cigarette. He coughed contentedly. He felt very happy, since alongside the real experience in the story about the watch he liked to give space to the imagination as well. For him everything had been, and still was, a project. He was not so much caught up in today. Instead he constructed himself in tomorrow. It was that way of dealing with life that had led him to join the armed struggle. For that same reason, on this Sunday, it was a treat for him to be in the midst of that group of children who were so quick and forced him to embellish the story of the watch with such details as had never before even passed through his head.

"And who did Fritz send the watches to in Portugal?"

"To some man named Silva, in Lisbon, who also made his living with watches. He bought them, sold them, repaired them, took out broken hands, and put in new hands."

It was delightful how the children laughed. They took part in the pretending, in that feeling that there was no dividing line between lived reality and re-created reality.

* Two figures in the MPLA list of heroes of the colonial war.

There was, indeed, a close link. Like the one that is always there between the sea foam and waves under the open blue of the sky. And in that link was all the sorcery made up of that mixture of dream and experience that Comrade Commander put into every word. Into every pause. Because what was really real was the story being told.

"One day, Mr. Silva sent to Angola many watches that the man from Switzerland had sold him—"

"What was his name?"

"Fritz. And that's how the watch in this story that's not really a story—since the things really happened—got to Luanda."

And the commander lingered awhile with that distant thought, in instantaneous recollection of every minute detail of the ambush, one of the high points of his entire life.

"And what was the watch like?"

"It was a fine watch. Expensive. And beautiful. It was gold plated and—"

"What is 'gold plated'?"

" 'Gold plated' is when a watch is gold only on the outside, as if it were painted with gold. But that is already good because gold is very valuable. Gold plating is like having the gold boiling in a pot and dipping the watch, which will then come out painted with gold." And the commander undid the band of the watch on his wrist.

"And where did Comrade Commander get that watch?"

"This one was given to me. Here in Luanda. But the other watch had gold hands, too, and didn't make even this noise (he held the watch up to the ear of one of the children), and these hour numbers lit up at night. It was luminous and had a calendar to keep track of the days, like this one. Oh! that's right, it also didn't need to be wound. It was automatic, like this one."

"And was the band the same also?"

"Yes, gold too. It was a fancy watch. A bourgeois' watch."

"Comrade Commander, didn't Gika have a watch?" And all eyes turned to the poster on the wall. To the hero's smile. Some of the children had even met him when he was here, with his jokes and stories, in this house by the sea.

"Yes, he did," answered the commander pensively. "Only in that picture you can't see it."

"What was Comrade Gika's watch like?"

The commander did something he didn't normally do when he told the story: he hesitated, seeming unsure. Memories rolled around in his mind, conversations about tactics and strategy, moments of happiness, or suffering, or discouragement. And with his eyes fixed on the ground he answered: "He had a special watch. It never broke down. You could even take a bath with it on. Even if the watch was hit, it always kept perfect time. Right on the dot. And it went around with our late comrade the whole time he was out in the bush."

He turned his head around and looked the poster up and down.

"But Valodia does have a watch on. What was it like?"

The commander hesitated. He lowered his head again, as though he were looking in the ground for roots he knew all too well. This one was harder to answer in any off-handed way. For Valodia had died right in Luanda. Right at the start of the big battles. And against the Chipenda forces.

"Yes, Valodia's watch was just like Comrade Gika's. Only . . . well, they had to have watches to know what time it was. . . . And they were two great comrades, even without watches," he concluded, somewhat abruptly. "But this story is about the other watch."

"And what about the other one?"

"The other one then came to Angola."

The children started shifting positions in eager antici-pation. Some moving an arm or a leg, others lying down, chin in hand, elbows on the ground. The story had now got to Angola!

"How did it get here, Comrade Commander?"

"It came along with other watches, because you never send just one watch for sale. Each watch came in a pretty little box, blue on the outside, with a spring catch. Velvet on the inside. And those little boxes came all together in a big box. Every big box contained at least two hundred watches."

"And how did they get here?"

"They came by boat."

"A big boat?"

"Yes. One of those big boats that can stay at sea a long time. It took them nine days to get here. Boats that have restaurants, electric lights, telephones, and zoom along like cars. The passengers travel up above in rooms called 'cab-ins.' Down below they put the cargo in storage areas called 'holds.' "

"Comrade Commander, take me to see one of those boats," asked one of the children, with his hand on his head.

"Only after independence."

"But Comrade Commander, you always say 'only af-ter independence.' Just the other time, when you told us that the watches came by plane and I wanted to go inside a plane, you said 'only after independence.' Why?"

The commander moved his leg. He took his foot out of the slipper. He laughed out loud and the children joined in. The stories about this story! One of the other times the watch had come from Lisbon to Luanda by plane. He stretched. He was very content this Sunday because the group was throwing out questions like never before. This was his greatest pleasure. To encounter every Sunday greater difficulties in telling the story of the watch. So that on sleepless nights, when his thoughts were stuck on his disabled condition, the commander could tell himself the story of the watch, all wrapped up in moonlight ruminations of children and sea. The story that he would later repeat was re-created in his own dreams. Also, the story would course through his blood with such appeal that when the morning sun had barely peeked through his window, he'd grab the crutches from the side of the bed, secure himself well with his other hand until he was in a sitting position, pull himself to his feet, and go quickly to the veranda, his mind stuck on only one thought: *I would love to know where that watch is now*. And he thought about time forgotten, looking at the roiling waters as if the sea contained all secrets in its waves and especially the secret of the story about the watch that he had worn on his wrist.

"But in the boat, inside the big box, did it make the noise that this one does?" inquired the child to whose ear the commander had placed the ticking watch.

"Yes, they were running when they left Switzerland. They were automatic."

The children looked at one another as if this time the commander were not only imagining but teasing them with tales. He understood. He lit another cigarette and proceeded: "You don't have to wind an automatic watch. All it needs is the motion of your hand, or the rocking of a boat. And a boat rocks plenty." But as the children looked dissatisfied, he continued: "They came into Luanda and were unloaded from the boat."

"But why did the watches have to come from Portugal?"

"Well, the watches had come from Switzerland. And from Switzerland to Portugal, and from Portugal they came to Luanda because watches aren't made in Luanda."

"But why aren't watches made in Luanda?"

The commander furrowed his brow. He cleared his throat and began twisting his beard with the fingers of his right hand, caught up in deep thought trying to come up with the best explanation.

"Many machines are needed to manufacture watches, and we still don't have those kinds of machines in Angola. And people who know how to operate those machines are also necessary. It is true that many things needed to make the watches come from here . . . " He was about to go into a more detailed explanation, but he felt powerless, foreseeing the detailed questions that surely would follow. He therefore started in on the voyage of the watch again: "They left the port. Have I already told you that the watches were shipped to the Paris Watch Boutique?"

"No. But what is this 'Paris'?"

"Paris is in France. It's the capital of France."

"Is it far away?"

"Yes."

"So why is that watch shop called Paris if it's here in Luanda?"

"Some stores take those names so that they seem fancier. This Paris Watch Boutique put the watches on sale in the *tuga* * PX here in Luanda."

The commander was finding it ever more difficult to respond to the questions that the children came up with. But deep inside him there throbbed the growing wish to keep hearing the children participate like this in the story. For the commander, the story had two faces. One was what he'd experienced in the forest. The other was all that greater beauty that the children brought to the plot. Details the commander hadn't thought of but which it would be

---

* A depreciative popular name for "Portuguese."

18

good to meditate on and establish ties with. In effect, the watch had its own trajectory. So a whole variegated gamut of situations passed through the commander's head, since the children posed questions nonstop. Who made the watch? Where had the watch been? All this was a way of humanizing it beyond its works, its hands, its band.

"And that—"

"Paris Watch Boutique—"

"—is where the watches were sold—"

"Yes. To the Portuguese army PX."

He took in all the children with his eyes, registering with that quick glance each expression, the intent, insatiable air, the position of their bodies. And the interferences in the narrative gave him the sensation that the story was always new and endless.

"Who here knows how to read?"

A child raised his hand: "Me!"

"Wait just a bit longer. After independence, when everyone knows how to read, we'll write the story and make a book out of it. All of us."

"And the watch?"

"The major bought the watch. In that Portuguese army PX here in Luanda. The owner of the Paris Watch Boutique gave a big discount so that the *tuga* soldiers could get the watches cheaper than at a store."

"But the major had come from Portugal!"

"Yes."

"So why didn't he bring his own watch from Portugal?"

"He did, but it broke. And since repairing it was almost as expensive as the price of a watch, he bought a new one. And also the soldiers had a mania for buying things. They would send some money back to Portugal and with what was left over they could buy things and take them home with them afterward."

"And did this major just stay in Luanda?" asked a child with the wide smile of someone who already knows the answer.

"No. And here comes the good part of the story. When he arrived he went to Grafanil. He was the second in command of the 193d Battalion. An infantry battalion."

"What's that?"

"Soldiers who fight with rifles, mortars, bazookas, and other things. They're ground troops, hand-to-hand combat if necessary. They don't have cannons. If they did they would be 'artillery.' Troops that bombard from planes are 'air force.' And those who attack from boats are 'navy.' "

"But the MPLA doesn't have an air force, does it?"

The commander looked up, measuring the span of sky: "We have to have an air force. After independence. You will be here with me to see our planes up above, tearing across our sky. It's going to be beautiful. And warships cutting proudly through that sea out there. And when that happens, you're going to be at the biggest party you can imagine."

The children asked questions with pleasure. Because they all understood in a general way these matters of infantry and air force. While some aspects of the war could be spoken of only clandestinely before, now, starting just a few months back, people of all ages would avidly put together a retrospective account of more than a decade of armed struggle. From the fourth of February to recent events in Kifangondo, with what had happened in the Baixa de Kassange in between, from the weapons used to the people who had died, stories of suffering and hope now traveled from mouth to mouth, stories in which the names of the heroes inevitably had to appear, like fireflies, unflickering and uncatchable in the long colonial darkness. But the children really loved it. They had an eagerness that allowed them to savor over and over things already known but made new in every detail through the commander's narration. Which he delivered as though he were breathing in a new air in that Luanda growing ever nearer to the childrens' famished eyes.

"And so? Did he leave here?"

"Yes. He was training commandos, which were a special force designed to infiltrate everywhere and kill many people. They would come into the villages just around sunrise. They moved a lot by night. They were handpicked. And they used tattoos."

"What are those?"

"Designs on their arms. You put a needle in some paint and then prick the skin with the needle—I heard a prisoner explain it once—and that's how a design is made."

"And was the major also a commando?"

"Well, he came as the second in command of the 193d Battalion."

"And what happened when they got to Luanda?"

At that point the commander raised his hand in a critical gesture: "A story doesn't go backwards, and I already said that they had gone to Grafanil." He lowered his voice, as if to go back and put the matter right. "Yes. When they got here they marched along the Marginal and after the parade the soldiers bought bunches of bananas."

The children burst out laughing. These were scenes etched in the memory of all Luandans. When the *tuga* soldiers disembarked, amazed at the cheap price of bananas, they stuffed themselves as if they were going to eat a lifetime's worth of bananas in one day.

"The major was in Luanda for eight months. Until he volunteered to head up the commandos at the front. He wanted to show what he was made of."

"And where did he go?"

"To the First Region."

"Where?"

"To the Nambuangongo zone. And here's where the story really starts to take shape."

"The story of the watch?"

"Well. Of the major. Who always wore that watch on his wrist."

It was almost a ceremonial juncture, as the children waited in wide-eyed anticipation for the story's next chapter. They all already knew the whole plot, but they knew as well that when least expected a new twist could be added. That always happened. Because they were all authors. The story belonged to everyone, a kind of painting that was being re-painted anew by the edge of the sea. There were even other collaborators: the lapping of a few little waves soaking into the sand adorned with shells and fine gravel; the dug-out canoes in the distance, plying the fishing waters; the tender noise of the wind combing the hair of the coconut palms. Then the commander lifted his head slowly, medi-tatively, his eyes glued to the sunlit horizon in order to keep being like the children around him: with the expectation that at that moment the story would again be told for the first time.

"The troops that the major commanded were being trained to finish us off. They set up quarters in Nam-buangongo. From there they planned to attack our base, which was some sixty kilometers away."

"And did they know where the base was located, Commander?"

"They had received some intelligence. They brought in some of the locals. Beating, torture, and the people talked. But whenever a person was taken in, someone else would be sent to warn us. So you see, we were prepared."

The children were delighted. Subjects directly linked to the war like that were the basis of the daily lives of most of the people in Luanda. But heard in this way, in the commander's voice, they were cause for even greater attention. And, too, they listened to learn. Even their games were war, making little slingshot rifles, setting up security at strategic points in the neighborhood, participating in, or even leading, military operations.

"And was there a road on which you could get to the base?"

"No. Only by cutting through the bush. And so it was necessary for them to take someone along, a guide who knew the way. But even so, the base was hidden down at a river's edge, under many trees." And he traced out the region's topography with his right hand. "There were two hills, one on each bank. We always had sentries stationed on the hilltops. So it was very difficult to assault our base. They even sent planes to bomb us. The bombs fell nearby but never damaged the base or killed anyone. The *tugas* were convinced that they'd been on target. During some periods of time they even seemed to think that we'd moved the base."

"And you never fired on any of the planes?"

"Oh, back then the base didn't have any antiaircraft weapons. Not to mention a lot of other things."

"And *monakachito?*"

That was one of the words most spoken by the children. An incredible marvel, the *monakachito*. In the conversations and discussions about the war it was a great failing not to know what a *monakachito* was.

"No, not one of them either. But look, the *mona* isn't good against airplanes. And listen now: the heaviest weapon then at the base was a bazooka."

"What kind?"

"RPG-7."

"And that was the time they were coming to attack the base, right?"

"Yes, but you all keep quiet for a while and don't stick in any more questions so I'll be able to tell everything in one piece and not forget some really beautiful part."

The children settled down again immediately. Coughing, stifling laughter, making faces, those who had pebbles and shells in their hands putting them down on the hard-packed earth of the veranda.

And only when silence was fully restored did the commander take up the story again: "We had some knowledge that the special troops led by the major were coming. They marched through the forest almost without noise. Well prepared for hand-to-hand combat. We increased the watch. And the base at reduced strength! Only thirty-four comrades. We had to be careful! But there were villagers nearby, only a few hours by foot. And they kept us completely informed. They knew where the *tugas* had been, boot tracks on the ground, tin cans, and sometimes at their patrol locations they left behind those cans and other remains of food, a lost or forgotten canteen, or a newspaper. The *tuga* troops had some information about us, then, but we knew almost everything about them. One day we got all the comrades at the base together. Our people were arriving with the news that the soldiers were patrolling the area and that their objective was to destroy our base. And that they knew everything: the best way in, the best time, our strength, because they already had beaten confessions out of one man. And people would actually tear up the soles of their feet running for kilometers, to arrive exhausted, sit down, and whisper as if the enemy were two feet away. And it really was true! Those guys were getting ready to dig our graves. So we met together. Conclusion: If the enemy is coming to attack us, and what is more, a special unit, well, we'll just have to find them first. So it was decided. We began to patrol with a great deal of caution, always using the most difficult terrain, and at times we would cross the path that our people said they'd be using. One day, a comrade arrived exhausted, his heart pounding, his feet bloodied from the zigzag run over the rough terrain, his body covered with sweat. He drank an entire gourd of water without stopping and then began to tell us some important news. It went like this—"

But a child interrupted, asking: "Did that comrade come right to the base?"

"Yes, to the base."

"So the people knew where the base was?"

"Of course. They were the ones who brought us food from their own crops, and when things got really bad all around, they came up close to us for protection."

There wasn't anyone there who didn't know every chapter of the story. But at the most exciting moments questions arose. It had become a ritual, that kind of page-turning to create an intermission whenever a juicy detail came up. And in this pretense of finding out what they already knew, they all played a part. Even the commander. Therefore the story didn't grow stale but rather seemed ever new, like the unknown time that was also renewed for every day of fear and hope lived in what was then a heroic and martyred Luanda.

"The man let it all out: that at *tuga* quarters they had made all the usual preparations. They had been holding five men, three women, and some children for more than a week. That our spies said they had heard some noncoms discussing an upcoming operation. That it was certain, the man said, it was really certain that they were going to force some of the prisoners to serve as guides. So we put two and two together. The night before, a plane had circled the base without dropping any bombs. A small plane. So there was no doubt: it had been on a reconnaissance mission. The man was telling the truth: the *tugas* had an operation in motion to attack our base."

"But they already had attacked the base, Comrade Commander."

"Yes, they had. But all the attacks had been big operations. Four of them. With air bombardment, long-range mortar fire, and shelling by artillery. We would keep a few men spread out around the base in the places where the enemy might come in and gather the rest in the bunkers."

"And then?"

The commander couldn't help but show a certain pride of knowledge and of triumph. "Then all we had to do was wait. The firing would stop. Hours would go by. They were convinced that everything was leveled. A few infantry soldiers would approach casually, talking out loud, careless. That's when we'd open fire on them. They took casualties and retreated, thinking our forces were much larger than their intelligence had indicated."

The commander expressed himself now with uncontained pleasure, and the children listened with such fascination that it seemed as if those victories had just taken place.

"And how did they try to attack this time?"

"This time it was different. They had at their headquarters these special troops that the major commanded. They were preparing a *golpe de mão*."

"A what, Comrade Commander?" interrupted one of the children, with a special note of curiosity in his voice.

"Well, I think I explained the other Sunday what that is. A *golpe de mão* is a surprise attack. Generally, it takes place in the early morning when it's least expected. These special troops come in like serpents, noiselessly. It would be like this: our comrades spend a calm night, no shooting; and in the early morning, when no one expects, the *tugas* just show up inside the base. With the big operations, you know everything ahead of time. Shooting and more shooting. People and more people flee to us with information to give. Planes dropping bombs. Who knows what all. But with the *golpe de mão,* watch out!"

"You mean, this time they were going to attempt a *golpe de mão?*"

"Exactly."

"And what happened?"

All the children clamored to change their positions, to move closer to the commander's chair, since at this point in the story complete and respectful silence ruled, like that of someone participating not in re-creating the plot but instead in the harshness and gravity of combat itself. And in those instances no one would stand for any confusion.

"Then we knew with absolute certainty. They were coming. There were fifteen of us dug in four kilometers from the base."

Unexpectedly, one of the children interrupted: "And who was in command of the fifteen comrades?"

"There were fifteen including me, and I was the commander. Besides that we had separate groups of three observing from the high points. The fifteen of us prepared our ambush. We dug foxholes. We stayed there for three days without any sign of the enemy. On the last night, most of the comrades wanted to return to the base because it seemed that the *tugas* had changed their plans. I, too, began to have my doubts that the enemy was going to attack. I even spent the night thinking about calling off the ambush and setting up patrols around the area. It could be that they were just doing careful reconnaissance so they could launch an attack later."

The commander paused briefly. He raised his head, lit another cigarette, and closed his eyes for a few seconds as though he were stopping at the best and most enthralling words in order to translate what his memory contained of that past as near as it was glorious. Then he continued: "It was around three in the morning. A Wednesday, I'll never forget it. The dogs from the nearby villages always barked when strangers came through. So when the *tuga* troops passed by the settlements—at night to avoid being seen—even though they kept their distance the dogs picked up the scent and barked. I checked everything out: each of the comrades was at his post. All on alert. From then on we listened intently. Not a sound could go by undetected. Half an hour later, we heard the dogs barking again, and since we knew the village locations by heart, we could tell by where the dogs' commotion was coming from that someone was approaching our position. The man who had come to our base had been right. They were coming!"

The commander took deep puffs on his cigarette and slowly let the smoke out in a spiral. He was no longer there. At that moment, all of his muscles were back in the foxhole. The blood coursed through his veins, and his mind was gripped with the determination not to let the intruders succeed in their plans to destroy the base and kill its inhabitants. Right now his cheeks seemed to be caressed by the cold of the morning *cacimbo*.* In his nostrils the smell of the earth. Here, in the little house at the edge of the beach, Comrade Commander held fast deep in the heart of the forest. He was at his post. He raised his right arm and pointed to the ocean with his index finger, like someone underlining the most important sentence of an open book about the ocean's waters: "We heard a sound that is easy to identify in the forest: metal hitting against something, a rock perhaps. It might have been a canteen or a rifle. None of us had any doubts. Our ears and eyes became even more vigilant."

* Early-morning drizzle or heavy dew.

28

The commander wasn't the only one who knew how to tell that magical story. The children did also. Everything was in order as if it had been rehearsed for a recital. Each and every word measured and placed at the precise time. Pauses always at the right moment. And, above all, that backdrop of sea and scalding sun with dugout canoes paddling against the tide looking for fish. Some people enjoying the beach's eddying water, others walking on the sand at the water's edge. Who would guess that on the veranda of that insignificant little house, with languid coconut palms swaying along with the rise and fall of the wind, Comrade Commander and the children were rewriting, repaginating, with enthrallment growing to crescendos, were bringing to an end that never ended that story more of love and hope than of hate and war that no writer would ever know how to put down on paper.

Quiet! The children didn't want to interrupt. Discipline of combat. They were all prepared for the ambush. Comrade Commander only had to give the order to open fire . . .

"It was half past five in the morning. Cold. The *cacimbo* had made our clothing wet. Our hands trembled. We began to hear the rustling of branches, leaves, grass. They were walking carefully to avoid making noise. Our foxholes were well hidden from view."

The commander twisted his beard and lowered his voice. "They came single file. At the front, the local man forced to be their guide. A soldier with a bazooka followed. After four or five others there was a soldier carrying a radio transmitter on his back with the antenna up." He stretched farther out across the chair and continued: "I let the local man move past the area where the last comrade was dug in, waited thirty seconds, and then opened fire."

The children stirred immediately, new positions for

their legs and arms. Now, yes! The ambush had begun in earnest. We are firing on the enemy!

"The shooting lasted about five minutes. Then they retreated, still firing. I regrouped the comrades. Not a single casualty. We retrieved five weapons and the radio. We could still hear shots in the distance and some bazooka and mortar rounds landing behind us, in the direction of our base. The enemy left five casualties on the ground. 'Move out comrades!'" And the commander extended his arm out. "I gave the order. We began to walk quickly, back in the direction of the base. It was necessary to reinforce other flanks because the enemy wouldn't be coming back through here now. It was also necessary to lift the morale of our comrades at the base, and of the people who had taken refuge there, with the news of this great victory. We had zigzagged through the bush for only twenty minutes when we heard a lot of firing at the ambush site. It was either the enemy reattacking the place, but too late, or else it was signal fire as they searched for their missing."

Honeyed smiles appeared on the children's faces. They smiled and joy brightened their eyes. A kind of flowery aura enveloped the commander, who at this point in the telling was not so interested in participating in the story line. What mattered was the victory; it was everybody's victory. That Sunday's victory, there on the veranda, each one with a rifle, all far away from the concrete reality, participating through imagination in the collective triumph: the success of the ambush.

"When we were almost to the base, a comrade came up close to me and said: 'Here, it's the major's watch.' The comrades wanted to surprise me. During the field reconnaissance they had identified the major among the casualties, but they waited until that moment to make the announcement and present me with the watch."

"The one from the beginning of the story?"

"Yes."

However far everyone's attention had wandered into the preparation for the ambush, the long wait, and its execution, once again they all returned to the initial theme.

"The one made in Switzerland?"

"Yes."

"The one dipped in gold and—"

"Automatic, you didn't have to wind it."

"And it had a light, kept track of the days, and didn't make any noise."

There it was, the whole watch, inside and out, in the children's memory! A watch that none of them had ever seen, but that they wore on their hearts' wrists during the ambush in which they all felt they were the commander.

"And the band?"

"I already told you. The band was like this one." And the commander dangled the band of the watch he wore on his wrist."

"And what happened to the watch?"

"Just hold on a bit," answered the commander, and he clapped his hands as if to call everyone to attention. "Before we get back to the watch, do you know what happened next? During that entire day we heard gunfire and explosions, and at night we saw some fires. It always happened like that. When the enemy suffered a defeat, they would fire on the near-empty villages as they retreated. They would destroy crops and burn houses. They took revenge on the people. It's true! Four days later, two planes came. It was a huge bombardment, but luckily, nothing worse happened."

"The watch, Comrade Commander?"

"Okay, let's move on."

Attention was rekindled, faces relaxed. They had left the foxholes at the ambush. The victors! The watch took up central position again. With all of its mechanisms. The luminous hands. The calendar. The gold plate. The band. And the adventure that lay ahead of it.

"I had that watch with me a long time. It became a trusted companion as well as a reminder of the ambush. We used it to keep track of the hours, days, and months. Only that very watch told us what time it was. The time back then!"

"But, Comrade Commander, tell us where you went afterwards and what happened to the watch?"

The child snapped that question out in a hurry to get to what he considered the high point in the watch's life. He wanted the commander to move on. But the others had surprise etched on their faces because the commander remained somewhat sad while he continued right on in a hesitant voice: "It's hard to talk about what life was like in the First Region after that time. At one point it seemed as if we were on an island. Surrounded. With almost no contact. I saw people falling down dead from hunger. No medication or food. Mothers forced to feed their babies on palm wine. The *tugas* always on the attack. Resupply all but impossible. Such times! Not many survived to tell about it!" And Comrade Commander raised his voice in such a way as to suggest that he had moved out of the story: "If there was resistance in this country, it was in the First Region. Resisting just to survive. There wasn't any clothing. We all had to go around naked. Here today, there tomorrow, sleeping like monkeys up in the trees. We couldn't even pay attention to the mosquitoes since they lit on us by the kilo. It's hard for me to believe it all. But after all we've been through, who can doubt that victory is certain? Is it or isn't it?"

"It is certain," responded the children in chorus. And the commander took advantage of the distraction, the shout of the official slogan, to surreptitiously wipe away

32

the tear rolling down his cheek. It was thick and heavy, like the terrible times in the First Region.

"One day a messenger arrived with an order from the comrades in command. We had to go into Zaire. To pick up weapons that other comrades had gathered together there. We could use the mission to establish contacts between the First Region and other points in the north of the country. Children, it's hard for me to talk about this! It was a long march. This part could be another story that one day we'll work on together here. But only after independence."

"Why, Comrade Commander?" interrupted the child who had already protested against putting things off until "after independence."

"Because that story is very long. It will take a lot of time. And also because it's a sad story."

The children stared at the commander's face, which had been happy just a short while before, manifesting the euphoria of the victory or examining again, from memory, the minutest features of the watch. But, at this moment, with furrowed brow, it revealed all the lines from more than a decade of combat.

"Then after independence, Comrade Commander, you will tell the story," concluded the boy who had disagreed with delays.

"Yes. But for now, I'll just say that thirty of us set out. Only ten were armed. Now look, only four of us made it to the banks of the Zaire River."

"And the others?"

"We lost them along the way. We went through six UPA attacks alone."

"So the others died?"

"Yes." And right there the commander reminded them: "I already said that it's a long story for after independence."

"But, just one thing."

"What's that?"

"Was that when you lost your leg?"

A special smile spread across the commander's face, filled with tenderness and love for the child's concern. It wasn't the first time. They almost always displayed that special curiosity and concern about how and why the commander had lost his leg. It was in that detail that he felt most important, realizing that the children understood that misfortune as one more glory to add to all the others.

"No. The leg happened here. On a mine twenty kilometers the other side of Caxito. You know where I mean? Comrades who fought for many years, who brought the war to Luanda, who spent the last months going all over the country, and—what horrible luck—lost their lives now, right at the end, right on the threshold of independence. Like Gika and Valodia."

All eyes moved to the posters. They had all heard words about independence and the MPLA victory right from the lips of Gika and Valodia, and they had, etched in their minds, the promises that the two commanders had made them about after independence. The sea, the sand, the lazy palm trees, and the sheltering veranda had been witnesses to those events.

"But Commander, the other Sunday you said that you were going to get a new leg."

"That's right. I am."

"When?"

"By next month."

"Where?"

"In a friendly country. Most likely East Germany."

"Then when you come back, you'll show us the leg."

All motioned their approval of the proposal with their heads, and the commander showed even more tenderness in his eyes and smile, approving also: "It's a deal. I'll show you the leg and I'll even teach you how to march."

The children clapped their hands.

"So now, do you want to hear the rest of the story about the watch that came from Switzerland and went so far, or not?"

"Yes, we want to," they answered in unison.

"Well, we arrived at the bank of the Zaire River on the border with Zaire. That is, on this side of the river it's Angola; on the other side it's Zaire. Some of our comrades were doing underground work there. They got ahold of a boat to get us across the river, and we made it without any problem. That night we slept on the other side, right at the river's edge. The next day, we set out on the march. Our comrades had gotten clothing for us—we were dressed as civilians, without weapons, and we went all over without anyone suspecting that we were Angolans from the MPLA. We had to go along the road for two hours. Then we were to go into the bush for another forty kilometers to our destination, where another group of comrades would be waiting. We barely got in half an hour."

"Why?" interrupted one of the children.

"A Zairian police patrol appeared in two Land-Rovers. They wanted to see our papers and asked about our nationality. We answered in French, said that we were Zairians, that we had been attacked and robbed of our money and papers. What's that? Those guys didn't believe us. The chief shouted he'd been warned that some people would be passing through, that we were all under arrest, and that this was no joke. He stank of alcohol, wetter than a baobob fruit, but we couldn't convince him. The encounter lasted for more than two hours. Two hours! He wanted to know what village each of us was from, and I invented stories for all of us, since I knew a little about the area. He asked about our jobs and again I invented for all of us: 'Peddlers.' Nah! He made us get in the vehicles. Then I said, 'Stay calm, don't start the engines up yet. I'm going to tell you the real truth. We're from the MPLA.' I explained everything: our struggle, the fourth of February, the First Region, our long march, the UPA ambushes. I told him that we were brothers, our people and his people were brothers. That that was the whole truth, and he couldn't arrest men who were fighting for independence. That this way we'd all die at the hands of the UPA in Kinkuzu. At one point, I could see in the comrades' eyes that they thought the police chief was being moved and would let us go in peace. But when I'd finished, the guy turned to the driver and gave the order to start the car. 'Wait!' I said. I pulled off my wristwatch. I gave it to him. He looked that watch over for at least twenty minutes. Then he asked, 'Gold?' I told him it was, and also automatic, luminous, made in Switzerland, the fancy watch of a Portuguese general killed in combat. I spoke with my hands on his and on the watch: 'It's yours, but you have to let us go in peace.' He ordered us out of the vehicles and didn't even say good-bye! They just left."

"And he took the watch?"

"Yes. The watch that was our companion for so long and that now we'd lost to save our lives. And here's the end of the story about the gold automatic luminous watch that came from Switzerland, that we won in an ambush, and that ended up on the wrist of a drunken police chief . . . not to mention corrupt."

"What's that?"

" 'Corrupt' means a person who sells himself, who lets himself be bought."

There was silence. The customary silence of disillusion that came when the commander closed the narrative. Such a beautiful watch, with so many twists in its plot, had, for the children, a sad ending to its life. It had traveled by boat, been taken from the wrist of the fallen major, and was finally lost on the other side of the border, precisely where the tyrants were now coming from to terrorize the Angolan people.

One of the children stood up and broke the ritual of silence at the end: "Comrade Commander, today the story can end another way."

"How?" asked the commander, surprised and perplexed at the boy's comment.

"Zairians are entering Luanda with the FNLA. And they set up a base in a *musseque*."*

"Which *musseque?*" another child wanted to know.

"Maybe Sambizanga," the first declared. Then he went on: "Then one night one of the lackeys leaves their base. Then he starts to walk through the neighborhood. Then he happens on a Young Pioneers base, and they see him and they grab him. He's taken prisoner. Then the *pioneiros* take away his gun and his watch. That gold watch that had been all over with Comrade Commander."

Resounding applause. The commander couldn't resist and he clapped hardest of all: "Very good. Today the story ends like that."

But the boy spoke again: "Then the *pioneiros* take the gun and watch to Vila Alice."†

"Very good," repeated the commander. "The watch returns!" And everyone clapped again.

Now the story had a different ending. And such was the desire that spilled out from the eyes and mouths of the children that it gave the impression that no one wanted, this time, to put a definitive end to the story of the watch. The watch that in each heart never stopped that automatic ticking, golden in dream and fantasy.

---

* One of the several shantytowns on the outskirts of Luanda. The term is sometimes extended to include working-class neighborhoods (Port.: *bairros populares*), although it does not have this meaning here.
† One of Luanda's working-class *bairros,* headquarters of the MPLA.

And with the commander already reaching to grab hold of his crutches, another child stood up with the air of someone who has climbed to the top of a tree and discovered the most beautiful, sweet, and succulent fruit: "Comrade Commander. That major we took the watch from, did he have children?"

"He must have had."

"Where?"

"In Portugal, where else?"

No one understood that interjection. So silence returned. Slow. Drawn out. The commander thinking that the child hadn't meant to take part in the actual story, that he'd jumped in only by chance. But the boy continued: "So, can I end the story too?"

"Yes. But, it's not exactly to end. It's to continue. The watch has already returned. And now?"

"Now the gun stays in Vila Alice. And the *pioneiros* go far away to the major's country. They're going to explain and take the watch back to his children." There was another bit of silence. A kind of meditation.

And only after the children had clapped loudly did the commander go along and clap as well, saying with unbounded satisfaction: "Very good. Today the story is more beautiful than on the other days! Hooray!"

"Hooray!" answered the chorus of children. And everyone stood up, satisfied with the ending.

But then one of them wanted to know: "Comrade Commander. And how are the *pioneiros* going to get there to take back the watch?"

There was laughter all around, since that was a problem they hadn't thought of.

Then, with a smile sweeter than the foam that kisses the sand at evening's end in Luanda, and eyes hotter with tenderness and affection than the sun when it slowly disappears, orange, behind the sea, the commander reached down and picked up one of the small shells on the hard-packed earth, put it in the palm of his other hand, and proclaimed: "The *pioneiros* will go in this shell, singing the MPLA anthem."

Joyfully laughing and jumping, one by one the children ran to the water and dived in, each in his or her special way.

The ocean was serene as always, there on that beach that extended a long way out. A children's beach. Blue transparent sea revealing a bottom with shells and conches beyond imagination. Then the commander took his crutches, walked slowly to the water's edge, and stayed there, in a draft of dreams and hope, taking in the sea and the horizon as if they were the beginning and end of the same story: the story about the watch.

The Last Bordello

They came in the back way. And, as was their custom, the
one in the lead gave a greeting in Portuguese: "Good
evening, 'sister.' "

Silence in return. Mana Domingas pretended that she
hadn't noticed them and went right on, her chubby face engrossed in the piece of plain-colored crocheting that she
had all but finished.

"You have that doily just about finished, Mana Domingas," one of the younger women said, by way of praise.
She was seated beside the small table on which sat the
record player and also the oil lamp with the shade on it,
which illuminated the room with a yellowish glow.

The proprietress sighed, still not raising her eyes from
her work, indeed, quickening a bit the speed with which
she twisted the threads. "Yes, my daughter; it is just about
finished."

The man who had come in first had his hands on his
hips, his legs apart in military posture. The other four
stayed back against the wall. All of them impeccably
dressed in uniforms, green, with new boots and Uzi automatic pistols across their chests.

"It's all sad in here tonight. Why?"

None of the women answered. From different parts of the room pairs of eyes focused complicitly on the heavy figure of the aged madam as she went impassively on with the rhythmic movement of her crochet hook.

He turned his head and stammered something in French to the other four. Mana Domingas paused surreptitiously in her crocheting. She peeked out of the corner of her eye, saw one of them step out from the wall, stick his thumbs inside his sagging belt, and answer in a highly irritated tone of voice. The old woman did not know French, but she gathered that the group suspected there was some sort of plot behind the silence. And they weren't liking it.

"We're not going to have any music?" the man in the lead started in again, openly scowling toward the table with the record player on it.

Again silence fell upon the room, to be broken by the proprietress's voice: "Milú, a glass of water please."

The young woman got to her feet and walked with her eyes glued to the floor. The man who spoke Portuguese tried to caress her neck with his hand. She drew back, responding, "Hey, take your hand off me; you can stick it you-know-where."

Mana Domingas pretended that she hadn't seen, and paused only to pull back apart a piece of her work in which she had made a mistake.

"So there's not even any music?" he asked again, now with a greedy look devouring the prominent breasts filling out the low-cut top worn by the girl sitting beside the record player. With one of her hands she smoothed out the doily that adorned the little table, and with the index finger of her other hand she began to trace sensuously its crocheted pattern.

"Beautiful crocheting, Mana Domingas. A wonderful job. But that new one you're working on, it could grace a wedding."

The madam profiled a smile of superiority, raised the water to her lips, took a swallow without showing any pleasure, and then sat the glass on the floor.

It was the only whorehouse left in the *bairro*. The one that had survived. When the Movement arrived, the populace had organized an offensive against prostitution. And, as if by a miracle, almost all the houses on the outskirts of Luanda disappeared. There remained only the fancy houses in the Baixa, which, under the cover of functioning as bars and nightclubs, went right on as in times past. It was in the neighborhoods that they had vanished. And some of the more unyielding of the prostitutes had not comprehended the change. They found the whole thing very strange. Men who knew their night life, from bordello to bordello, now passed them by with disdain, wrapped up in what they called "people power" and "neighborhood committees." There were others who even spat on the ground in disgust, and, among the women, the greengrocers who had their stalls in the area started refusing to sell tomatoes or onions to any female who, by her dress, walk, or perfume, signaled that she made her living by selling her body.

But Mana Domingas's establishment had held on! It had been the most expensive, and most frequented, in the area—in fact, in competition with the best in all of Luanda. A truly elite house! With carefully picked girls, well kept, dressed in provocative miniskirts, high heels, blouses with less cloth than the skin they revealed; and they were always engaging, active in serving drinks, changing records, going back and forth to the rooms. The house had gained its notoriety through its high prices and distinguished clientele of important people from that part of the city where the streets were paved: captains and majors in the *tuga* military, doctors, engineers, and even a doctor of law, head of the judiciary, who, in his passion for one of the prostitutes, had lived there in scandal with that woman whose name in fact appeared on the police register.

A house of repute, with Mana Domingas in charge.

Then the MPLA *Delegação*[*] arrived. And the various houses of assignation began their almost natural decline.

At the same time, the puppet forces began locating military bases all over Luanda. They dug in in this neighborhood, convinced that since the majority of the inhabitants here came from the north, they could transform it into a kind of headquarters for terrorism. Then they discovered Mana Domingas's house, which, increasingly estranged from the neighborhood people and deprived of its accustomed revenues, took in these new clients with open arms. And they protected the house. They even set up security, impressing upon the girls' minds the notion that they were indispensable, since one of these days "people power" might come in and ruin everything.

Then began the repression of the neighborhood people. Mainly of anyone suspected of being an MPLA militant or sympathizer. People Mana Domingas had known from birth on. Now she would hear that they had been found with their bodies riddled with bullets, limbs cut off. There were even stories of "serious" girls, only twelve or thirteen years old, being raped under threat of violence.

But they came. They brought money. They kept the bar stocked. And Mana Domingas tolerated them. With the result that neither madam nor any of her girls dared walk through the area, so great were the rejection and the hostility they encountered on the faces of each and every person. The clients themselves ended up having to bring in

[*] The reference is to the organized presence of the MPLA. The *Delegação*, located in Vila Alice, was one of its headquarters buildings.

the food. The food that was so scarce in this Luanda at war.

So Mana Domingas, after the phase of receiving them as grand clients had passed, now tolerated them with a mixture of fear, hatred, and resignation.

The one who spoke for them all insisted, now with authority in his voice: "Music, 'Sister' Domingas!"

The old woman raised her magisterial head, hands folded, the crocheting spread out in her lap: "We can't, the needle broke." And, lowering her head back down like a dead weight, almost to the point where she touched the hook and thread with her eyes, she started in on her work even faster than before.

He went back to speaking French. The other men responded with a raucous laugh, and one of them pulled a pack of cigarettes out of his pocket.

First he held out the cigarettes to the girl next to the record player. She didn't want one. Then he started making the rounds of the room. There were eight girls in all. One by one they turned him down. They shook their heads and either thanked him or simply said no. He finally walked across the room and held the cigarettes out to Mana Domingas. The old woman didn't even thank him. She very convincingly pretended she didn't even see him. The soldier put on a forced smile to compensate for his lack of success and droned something in French.

"Mana Domingas, when are you going to finish that piece? You started it a long time ago," asked one of the girls, who wore a tall wig and whose lips were heavily painted with brown lipstick.

"I'll finish when God wills it."

"And if He doesn't will it?" kidded another one, tongue-tied.

"God always wills, my child," aphorized Mana Domingas, sweat beading on her face, "God always wills . . . "
And she let out a deep sigh, her breasts rising almost high
enough to touch the fat of her chin.

The soldier who spoke Portuguese sat down in one of
the easy chairs upholstered in blue imitation leather. He
placed his weapon on the floor. The others remained standing, in a constant, patient surveillance of the girls.

There was something strange, free-floating in their
look. The bordello was different today. Quiet. No music,
no laughter. The madam's attitude and the girls' behavior,
too, were totally different from normal.

They hadn't accepted business for almost three days
now. It was a time when war was raging in the neighborhood between the FNLA and the people. Three days in a
row. Shells shaking the ground, landing on top of houses.
Weapon fire pouring out from anywhere and everywhere.
During that period the proprietress ordered the doors kept
closed, the curtains tightly drawn, and only occasionally
would she send one of her employees out to take a careful
look around. People running in all directions. Individuals
passing by outside the door in tears and with cries of anguish. Some had saved small possessions and were carrying
them on their heads, the women always cursing the disaster of not at least being able to recover the bodies of family
members or look for the missing.

Today, at nightfall, the conflict had abated. An occasional shot or volley could still be heard, but that alone
didn't frighten anyone. Because that was the way the
bairro had been since the puppet soldiers had set up their
installation here.

"Who's running the larder today? Give us some beer
to celebrate. Let's toast!"

No response. So he spoke louder, clapping his hands
together: " 'Sister' Domingas, beer!"

The madam stopped her crocheting for an instant, answering without even altering the position of her head: "There is no beer." And she went on wielding her hook as if nothing had happened.

Flashes of fear shone on the girls' faces because of the boldness of Mana Domingas's response.

"That is right, isn't it, Mana Domingas? No more beer comes into this house."

"Yes, it is, my child," said the proprietress, this time raising her head to give a look of gratitude for the girl's attempt to help her out of this awkward situation.

He stood up and went back to jabbering with the other men in French. They spoke loudly, gesticulating with their arms. Mana Domingas could not hide an air of concern, convinced that were discussing what was taking place, the strange and unusual manner of their reception. She stopped her crocheting and started to move her lips in a silent prayer.

But just as she began, the soldier who spoke for them all walked across the room with long strides, shoved aside the prostitute who happened to be in his way by pushing her shoulder, and banged open the pantry door. The other men burst into laughter.

Mana Domingas and the eight girls stiffened in a silence of frozen dread as they heard the noise of the refrigerator opening and counted, one after another, the tinkling of the bottles. Then the man came back to the door and beckoned to the others to come in. The girl seated near the door pushed her chair farther away, to avoid more collisions.

Every man brought out beers, three in each hand, holding their necks between their fingers. Then the leader came back out of the pantry with an entire case, which he held vertically and then dropped onto the floor beside the chair he had been sitting in. He spoke in French, and one by one the others went back into the small room.

When they heard the noise of the refrigerator crashing flat on the floor, Mana Domingas took her hands off her crochet work and raised her head, her trembling eyes fixed on the open door. The girls remained silent. They focused their gaze on the madam's eyes, to see if they could discover from her a means of putting an end to this calamity. None of them was attentive to the goings-on in the pantry: the sounds of kicks and hammering pistol butts falling on the refrigerator, glass being shattered, shelves being pulled out, tins and bottles falling to the floor in pandemonium. They heard it all quite distantly.

When she saw the first soldier come back into the room, the proprietress automatically lowered her head and took up her crocheting again. But she couldn't concentrate; she merely went through the motions. The hook in her right hand did not engage the linen thread, nor did the other hand feed it in. She was constructing a kind of imaginary crochet work with an agitated trembling of her jowels, chin, and arms.

The soldier opened a beer with his sabre. Three of the men did the same after him. The last one chose to use his teeth.

The girls kept their eyes glued to the floor.

The soldier gulped the beer down in a single swallow, raised the empty bottle high in his right hand, and turned to the others to get their attention. Then he aimed a smile toward the madam of the house as though he were about to offer a toast: "You old whore! Catch!"

Mana Domingas barely had time to duck as the bottle whistled over her head and flew through the glass window before shattering on the ground outside. Even after that Mana Domingas went on engaging in her threadless crocheting with her hands, tears welling out of her eyes.

"Common whore!" And with his left hand he gestured toward the metal point of his sabre. "Only respect for the 'sisters' here keeps me from running this up your ass!"

The madam couldn't control herself any longer and broke down in grotesque sobbing, the crochet work, the hook, and her hands over her semitoothless mouth.

"So you whores are hiding beer now, huh?" and he launched another empty bottle, this time against the ceiling, and the girls ran terrified out of the way to avoid the shower of falling glass.

Then there began what was for the men the high point of this entertainment. They drank beer after beer, throwing the empty bottles against the walls in a game in which they watched and laughed as the prostitutes ducked the flying glass. The man who spoke Portuguese was the only one who didn't join in on the breakage. He remained lost in thought, looking at Mana Domingas, who, once in a while, glimpsed with her eyes an occasional spark in his. She experienced there moments of short-lived but profound victory. None of her employees had given in and done what these men expected: get up and sue for peace with arms of flesh, passionate smiles, and sex.

"If it wasn't for the girls, I'd run this up your ass, you rotten old bitch. You can bet I would!" And he belched as he repeated in French what he had just said, for the benefit of the other men.

The proprietress took up her crocheting once more, the hook reengaging the thread. The parade of bottles against the wall had ended, and the madam was inciting the visitors' ire with her haughtiness. She organized herself as she had been at the outset: pretending that she was alone and absorbed in her crochet work.

Then the one who had been acting as interpreter threw himself in a fury against the semicircular piece of furniture that served as the bar. The glasses made a clinking noise as they broke against the concrete. He grabbed hold of one of the giraffe-foot benches and, with infuriated pounding, tore apart the piece of furniture from which the prostitutes usually served drinks to their clients.

Suddenly, there came from outside the sound of a shell exploding. Then another one—and single-shot weapon fire.

The group of men exchanged looks. They traded more words in French. Mana Domingas gleaned, with satisfaction, from their tone of voice that they were now in a hurry to leave. She hadn't learned much in the way of French, but from the rhythm and intonation of their utterances she could guess the sense of the conversations. They were now hurrying to divide up the girls.

"Hey, Sophia! You go into the room with this *frère* . . . this 'brother.' And he pointed with his right index finger to the prostitute wearing the brick-colored *bubu* in a mask print. He was now thoroughly drunk and he gave orders like a general at a military parade: "With . . . this . . . *frère!*" he slowly repeated, emphasizing each word.

"But I cannot," answered the girl, pasting a falsely sweet, experienced smile on her face.

"Why?"

"I just got it today." And she proclaimed moralistically: "It's fate."

The leader turned back with a sidelong glance to the other man involved. Mana Domingas understanding that he was explaining things to the other man, who at the same time was nodding his head and searching over the room with his eyes, until he fixed his lust upon the big girl with the huge eyes who wore green bell-bottom pants and a miniblouse that covered just a bit of the lower part of her breasts.

"Guida, you go into the room with the 'brother.' "

She stood up slowly, theatrically, having first glanced over to authority in the figure of Mana Domingas. Swaying her hips with practiced provocativeness, with her left hand she let down erotically her long, loose, smooth hair, holding her chins with her right.

"You're going to have to leave me out, pal. When the fighting's over, I'm going to have this tooth pulled. I have what you call an 'abscess.' Say, maybe your army pharmacy has some *milongo* herb you can get me for it."

The madam traveled through her almost-forgotten crocheting with a splendid calm painted on her face for the girls to see. There was no further sound until the visitors began to dialogue in French again.

Mana Domingas paid even greater attention to the tones of voice. There was no doubt: they were arguing and, in the midst of a serious difference of opinion, were looking for the most practical solution. At that point, the man who spoke Portuguese, staggering in his drunkenness, went over to the slender girl in the jeans who had her elbows resting on the small table with the record player on it.

"You go."

The young woman remained absolutely still, the soldier staring at her with a domineering look. He walked over to her and shook her by the shoulders: "Let's go; do what I say. Into the room—now!"

"I won't go." And with a twist she pulled herself back out of his grip.

"Who says you won't go?"

"I'm the one who gets to say, and I won't."

And she kept on, her elbows pressed to the tabletop, her head hanging suspended between her hands.

She was the newest prostitute in the house, aspired to by all the clients but the hardest to get, because Mana Domingas would set the price very high. And she would hold firm. Without vacillating.

The spokesman now began walking about the room, kicking the bottle shards, trying to intimidate the girls, who, in contrast, continued to manifest a sublime indifference.

The refrigerator had been completely destroyed and now was good for nothing more than scrap metal. The pantry had been torn apart, cans and jars of macaroni, rice, salt, and other condiments all heaped together on the floor along with fragments of glass from the jars, and beer soaking it all. The semicircular bar and high stools had been reduced to kindling. These objects of food, drink, and ornament were what was of greatest value to these women who earned their livelihood by selling themselves. He could not, therefore, understand the girls' behavior. Tonight an atmosphere of tension floated through the room. They seemed to be at a wake for someone they had hated in life. Neither bottles thrown over their heads nor falling glass nor any of those other things had moved them.

In the midst of such thoughts, standing in the middle of the room, under the careful scrutiny of Mana Domingas, he fixed his eyes again on the young girl. The table, the record player covered by a doily crocheted by the proprietress's own hand. In a sudden burst of rage, he pulled off its glass cover and threw it against the wall.

"Today we're going to end up torching all this crap!" And he ripped the arm off the record player.

The girl remained impassive. She seemed to be half-asleep.

The men exchanged more words in French. Their rage was obvious; they spoke very loudly, evidencing a certain clash of opinion. Mana Domingas raised her head up with greater calm. The experience of year after year in the whorehouses had instilled in her an inner hope: these men, drunk, the alcohol going to their heads, might end up canceling each other out in their confusion.

Not a shot was to be heard. The night seemed about to yield a miraculous calm after the last three days of conflict. Three days of terror during which Mana Domingas had prayed like she had never prayed before. But at this moment, seeing the house torn apart, its contents all smashed, the madam found herself praying for the war to come back. With whole volleys of bullets. And mortar rounds. Yes, that was the salvation. She knew these men well. If the firing came again in earnest, they would leave on the run, each in a different direction. So Mana Domingas, eyeing the figure of the leader as he weaved back and forth on his feet, went on meticulously forming the stitches in her crocheting.

He coughed, sucking in the spit, almost choking. He wiped his mouth on the back of his hand and then pulled a wad of crumpled bank notes out of a hip pocket, growling, "It's money, isn't it? With you whores it's always money. Well, there it is!"

He became exasperated. He expected to see one of the prostitutes leap up and grab at the money—especially the young girl—but none of the women even so much as looked at the notes scattered on the floor.

Desperate, he threw himself upon the young girl. He stuck his hands down inside her blouse to grab her breasts. She rose up like a spring, flung out her arms, screamed, and, struggling to free herself from the hands that were squeezing her breasts, defended herself by sinking her teeth into the aggressor's arm until he released her.

"I'm not going into that room!"

"Why?" he asked, his drunken eyes staring at the wrist pitted with wounds from the prostitute's teeth.

"Why? I asked." And he hit her, hard.

"I'm not going to bed with any French speakers!" the girl said, now somewhere between tears and sobs.

It was as though the roof had fallen in. Mana Domingas almost stopped breathing. He took his hands off the girl and stopped for a lucid instant, thinking, his head down in shock. This time he didn't translate for the others.

"But then you'll go to bed with *me*. If you don't, you're going to see what an ELNA soldier is made of. An ELNA soldier!"

"Take your hand off. I'm not going to bed with anybody; I've left the business. Get away from me!"

"But I speak Portuguese." And saying that he grabbed her by the arms and tried to pull her with him. "Let's go. Pick up the money. All of it! All the money."

"I'm not going. Leave me alone."

"But I do speak Portuguese," he insisted. He made an effort to pull the girl with him. He got her up and with one hand ripped off her blouse. Her breasts were left bare, taut and adolescent. The prostitute, in a virginal gesture aimed at preserving her integrity, covered herself with her arms, leaned back with every iota of strength she had, and burst out with the sobbing words: "I'm not going to bed with . . . murderers!"

Mana Domingas stopped her work and remained motionless, the hook suspended in her right hand, seeking a thread in the air. The crocheting fell to the floor. There was a brief glimpse of the sabre blade gleaming within the sculptural brilliance of the young woman's breasts in the yellow light of the lamp with the shade, her cry as she fell over on top of the table, the crash of the lamp to the floor, and then darkness everywhere. The madam leapt up and with sure fingers felt for the door latch.

Once outside, she ran, panting crazily, until she reached the start of the asphalt pavement.

There was no other safe route to use in fleeing. Behind were only enemies. Either random shooting—never, at night, aimed at any intended victim—or the well-known rampant rapes on the part of the ELNA soldiers, or shame and deprecation before the neighborhood people. No, this was the right path: into the great anonymity of the city.

There, before her in the dark, at the entrance to the avenue, Mana Domingas glimpsed some familiar figures. She went another hundred meters forward, the superfluous crochet hook still clutched nervously in her right hand. She hadn't even shed a tear.

Three of the girls were there. Silent. At this, the only practicable point of meeting and of flight.

The proprietress looked back again to where they had come from, but when she heard the echoes of automatic weapon fire followed by the explosion of a grenade, she took a definitive step onto the pavement.

There was no doubt. The sounds were coming from the bordello.

They then began walking, single file, hurriedly. They walked along the right side of the street. Without saying a word.

At one point they saw a group of people on the other side of the street walking in the same direction. Four women were carrying bundles on their heads. An old man with a child on his shoulders. Two men. And a young man in front, with a weapon in his hand.

Mana Domingas started across the road diagonally, followed by the three girls. The people on the other side stopped their progress.

When the madam got close to the young man at the head of the line, she asked: "Where are you going, comrades?"

The militiaman came up close to the old woman. He studied that face so widely known and talked about in the *bairro*. And after being sure, he spat in repugnance: "Aha! So now you are comrades? Since when?"

"Yes, we are, comrade."

Mana Domingas was trembling. Two thick tears now rolled down from her eyes, but she stifled her sobs by squeezing the superfluous crochet hook deep into her right hand.

Two more grenade bursts were heard, and they all turned their heads toward the source of the sound. It was Mana Domingas's house.

The young man's eyes remained fixed indecisively on the old woman's fat face until the tall flames began to lick up into the night. Another house on fire. The house that had belonged to Mana Domingas. The last bordello.

The old woman smiled. She touched with her fleshy hand the hot face of the young man whom she had known since he was an infant, measuring in her memory the time gone by during which he had grown, and she asked: "Where are you comrades going?"

"We're going to Vila Alice, to try to get weapons."

"Then we'll go too."

And as no one in the group raised an objection or made a comment, the young militiaman gave with a gesture a sign to recommence the march.

The single line had grown. One of the girls carried her yellow high-heeled shoes in one hand. Mana Domingas was walking along barefoot. And when she instinctively raised her hand to her throat and felt the gold choker that another Zairian commander had given her when the fighting had first moved into the city, she undid the cord, weighed it in her hand, walked along a few more paces with the gold clutched in her right hand, and then, without anyone seeing, let it fall into the grass that grew along the edge of the street.

The night was enveloped by the usual freshness of the sea breeze, and, in the sky, some stars shone, while the silence seemed to promise a hiatus in these disastrous times.

But a few tracers painted the space between Avenida Brasil and Vila Alice. A space of life or of death. With Mana Domingas walking along, her superfluous crochet hook still tightly clutched in her hand.

Two Queens of Carnival

It's hard to believe. All I can do is just put my hands up to my head. Should I pray or not? It's going out of fashion; they say it isn't revolutionary, it doesn't look good. But I really need to say a prayer. To say I don't know exactly what, or scream out loud, ask the questions of other people, find out how it happened, clap my hands, sing, dance, or—I swear—pick up a can of red paint and a paintbrush and go around painting on all the walls. But painting what? Painting precisely: "It's hard to believe." "How could it have happened?" This joy people have in making it known that they have lit hell afire and that joy itself has fire in it. The total hell that was that yesterday no one will ever forget. Worse than after the assault on the prison. Fourth of February! People still have to scratch their arms, bite their lips, stomp on the hot earth with their feet, open and close their eyes over and over again to be sure in their bodies that they really are awake, that they are seeing what there is to see, that they still have the burnt smell in their noses and can hate all over again. Yes, hate! To have pass through your veins the urge to grab a mattock and take as long as it takes to bring down those walls that are now all blackened by the bombardments but that continue making you remember those days when the taste of death was measured in every move. The taste of death! And of terror. Preceding death.

The building, originally blue, is all smoke-discolored. On the lower floors all that is left of the windows are the iron frames, pulled out of the walls. Scattered around, whole piles of rubbish. Fragments of building material, broken glass, metal beams, sheet metal, pieces of tables, chairs, semidestroyed photocopy machines, publicity fliers, all thrown together in a heap as though it had all tried — unsuccessfully — to flee. The only thing missing was a flag. Yellow, red, and white flags, not even with all the sophisticated machinery brought in from America, from Zaire, from France, from Germany, from England! Volleys of fire had been directed here. Mortar rounds fell here. Artillery fire landed here. Then, while the gunpowder smell was still rising into the air and news ran from mouth to mouth among the people of Luanda and the soldiers of the people raised their weapons in victory, not even they could hold back the march of the people, the strength of the people, who also came through here, with arms waving and well-known organized songs. And did the people come through here! Pillaging trophies. Half-burned chairs. Tables in a similar condition. Pieces of typewriters. Electric cords. Chains from flush toilets. Empty whiskey bottles. Pieces of carpeting. Floorboards. Hangman's ropes. Lamp parts. Refrigerators beaten into figure eights that would never work again. And also halves of things that the person who had them didn't even know what use they had served or what any further use might be. It didn't much matter, for the value or utility of the things wasn't the issue. What was vital was to have something in your hand, anything, taken from the puppet base. The *pioneiros* were the ones who sorted through the junk piles looking for defective firearms, pipes, and reusable wood to make their slingshot rifles with. They comb through the wreckage carefully with their feet. Wherever there's a mound of debris, burned wood, and ashes, you'll find them there: digging around with a stick in search of unexploded munitions.

All of a sudden, Umbellina stopped responding to the order words.*

Her feet felt as heavy as lead; the blood ran cold in her veins. Her skin grew clammy in a chilly sweat. She raised her hands to her mouth, and while tears ran down her cheeks, she tried to stifle her sobs.

She had come on foot. Almost no one was at work at the Palace today; for all practical purposes the offices were closed. The news of the victory had been known since early morning. In the afternoon, Umbellina and two other ministry cleaning women were talking in the hallway, next to the PBX desk, when a call had come in about some of the missing and dead. There were always people ready to bear the information, check all the hospitals and morgues, attend all the funerals. Umbellina was a part of that network.

She hurried to finish her cleaning, left in a panic at seeing the hundreds of people that the FNLA was beginning to push toward the periphery of the Palace district and into the Saneamento neighborhood, listened to a comrade who worked as a messenger warn her that the BJR was working in the area, and then lumbered heavily along a prudent route to the morgue.

It was true. Kito's body was there. With a sort of look of surprise frozen on his face!

Then, back outside, she found herself enveloped in

---

* Albeit awkward, a more or less direct translation of the Portuguese *palavras de ordem*. The term refers to the phrases used by MPLA followers to express their dedication and resolve, maxims for each MPLA follower to live by. They also served as public slogans.

this mad wave of running bodies. Everyone wanting to see the places the defeated enemy had occupied. Streets, places where it had taken great courage just to go before. For Umbellina, to go along would simultaneously be to forget about the morgue. A kind of compensation.

She resisted no longer. Then, in the next instant, she separated herself from the collective euphoria, came back to herself, felt herself bearing Kito's memory — the respect, the grief, of both his mother and his *bairro*. She should have run immediately to notify neighbors, the comrades on the neighborhood committee, so they could comfort Comrade Mimi with the customary care, relieving her of a portion of the pain on hearing the news that she had a son in the morgue.

That was certainly her duty, because at this very moment comrade Mimi might well be one of those making the satisfying pilgrimage through the destroyed puppet bases, no one having told her of the tragedy.

And Umbellina poured out in tears and sobbing the memory that had immediately come to her when, that short time ago, she had seen Kito, a corpse in the morgue: one day, in the morning, when he affectionately insisted, "Auntie, today you're going to ride on the motorcycle." The sensation of the morning breeze whipping across her face at the speed of the motorcycle, with her holding on so tightly that he finally had to tell her that it was dangerous.

It was really her duty to be in the *bairro*. Talk to the neighbors. Help with the preparations for the funeral. Be with Comrade Mimi. *God Almighty! Where else on the earth have happiness and despair come together so often? On the same day. In the same place. It's hard to believe! Will this be our fate forever? For how long, then? My God Almighty! I can see you now, Comrade President, arriving at the airport. I watched you from a distance because they wouldn't let me get any closer. But you said so many times that this was going to change, the people were to be free, no one in fear, new things were coming,* pioneiros *in school with books, slates, uniforms, everything paid for by the state, because everything would belong to the people. No! It can't be our fate forever! But now Kito is dead! A lot of people are dying. But Kito always talked about the MPLA. All the time. His mother, Comrade Mimi, talked about nothing else but the MPLA. The whole* bairro *talked about nothing else but the MPLA. He was in the militia. In the last confrontation, barricaded with five other men behind drums filled with sand, he stood up to the thugs' fire, helping the* bairro *hold out against them. He was a hero! But who knew about it? No one wrote a song about him, and his picture wasn't put up on building walls. My God! To die—like that!*

What's going on? Talking to yourself and still crying, even now, at a time like this? Let's get up to the head of the procession!

A young man, one of the leaders of the euphoria, grabbed Umbellina by the arm. For a few moments people focused their gaze on the sobbing Umbellina, thoroughly convinced that it was pure joy that made her cry that way.

At that point, a young woman in a miniskirt and double-high heels, who was singing and dancing, lifted the Afro wig off her own head and arranged it on Umbellina's. "We have a queen!" she proclaimed, and Umbellina redoubled her tears, her sobs; she put her hand forcefully into the young man's hand, pulled him into the middle of the avenue, and started shouting: "THE M-P-L-A IS THE PEOPLE; THE PEOPLE ARE THE M-P-L-A." The crowd answered back in a frenzy, voices coming from deep down inside, everyone shouting "THE M-P-L-A IS THE

PEOPLE; THE PEOPLE ARE THE M-P-L-A." The entire procession started up the avenue.

Cars accompanied them, keeping the beat with their horns. Some of the people had already gone up the street and come back down again. Others had been going about their daily chores and now joined the procession that Comrade Umbellina was leading, at this moment with her heart only smiling.

"Who *is* that comrade?" asked someone in one of the front rows.

"I don't know. But look at the numbers she brings in. She really knows how to bring people together!" concluded a young man with books under his arm.

With the mass of humanity ever ready to respond with fervor to the order words, Umbellina, elected by popular will to lead this procession, felt a singular satisfaction in that leadership position. To utter two or three words and have all those people respond! To say "This way, comrades" and have everyone go in that direction was in fact something new and remarkable for her.

"To the right," said someone. "Let's go toward Avenida Brasil."

And Umbellina, accepting the suggestion, turned her entire retinue right.

They came into the small plaza that gave access to Vila Alice. The FAPLA patrol stationed there didn't even inquire who the revelers were and where they were going. They were the people! Hands on cartridge clips, they raised their weapons euphorically skyward. The multitude waving its arms with fingers in a V sign! Umbellina shouted at the top of her lungs: "Long live the FAPLA!"

"Long live the FAPLA!" responded the crowd in unison. And a collective volley echoed from all the weapons' clips.

"Down with the *kazukuta!*"* criticized an old woman half-frightened by the shots.

"It isn't *kazukuta;* it's victory, comrade!" responded one of the soldiers, his arms open wide as though to embrace a sun made brand new.

"VICTORY! VICTORY! VICTORY!" screamed the crowd, quickening its pace.

Dust rose up from the unpaved road, and more and more people joined that spontaneous procession commanded by Umbellina, who, now completely absorbed in her role as queen, would now and again shake her Afro wig.

Some people who had paused in indecision about joining the celebration finally could resist no longer and gave the first indications of how their hearts felt with bottles that they had found in the refrigerators at one of the lackey bases. "They're there at the SAM† for all the world to see. We have to kill every one of those assassins!" Then they quickened their pace with the goal of getting into one of the front rows of people. Those more reticent in this sort of situation let the others go ahead so they could fall in at the end.

When Umbellina looked to the left, she was surprised: the column now had a FAPLA escort. She shifted her eyes to the right, here in the heart of the Cidadela, the bastion that the lackey forces had chosen as the area from which to machine-gun the people, and on that side as well, along the shoulders of the road, a line of soldiers was escorting the celebration. "Long live the FAPLA! Long may it live! THE

---

* Originally the name of a wild Angolan dance, it describes a state of disorder or confusion. Here an approximate translation would be "hooliganism."

† Medical Assistance Services (Serviços de Assistência Médica), a medical aid station.

M-P-L-A IS THE PEOPLE; THE PEOPLE ARE THE M-P-L-A." And, with that shout singing of the joy of victory, Umbellina broke into a run, and the crowd followed.

The buildings, with their windows shattered and the walls pockmarked from the shelling, revealed this as one of the areas of bitterest fighting. All you had to do was turn the corner. Avenida Brasil was right there in sight! The shouting of the order words came faster to match the quickened pace that Umbellina had imposed upon the march.

That's what the MPLA was about. In joy or in sorrow the people came from everywhere. Like a great river at full flood. People who didn't know one another spoke of their sorrows and misfortunes. Minute details of private lives were confessed, and at a time when food was as scarce as gold and half of downtown Luanda was getting by on canned goods obtained by waiting in long lines, after an MPLA conversation, comrades who were complete strangers might invite us into their homes and set before us a hot meal with all the trimmings. The people were organized! Tomatoes, completely absent in the city, were to be found in the outlying *bairros* and in the *musseques*. *Fuba** and palm oil, unavailable on the asphalt, were also to be found there. And people identified themselves as though they had known one another for years. It was almost impossible for a lackey to infiltrate the ranks of the MPLA. The MPLA people had their procedures for any case that might arise. In conversation, there were the allusions: Comrade So-and-So on the neighborhood committee, Comrade Commander of that base, the number of lackeys downed, a make of firearm for every distinctive weapon sound, commentary on the "Angola at War" radio program, or knowledge by heart of the order words and the revolutionary

---

* *Fuba* is a flour made of mixed grains and tubers.

hymns; and, if it became necessary, there was even code language, sign and countersign. So that when enemies tried to engage in espionage amid the people, they were almost always hung out by the fingernails. Because all that it took was one summary interrogation to discover that this was an infiltrator.

The formation changed, shortening and widening out to take up the street's full width. As a result, automobile traffic was blocked. Today, Avenida Brasil belonged to the people. A street by now already storied. Many, many people had died along it because the lackeys made a habit of shooting for the fun of it. Sometimes, even as they called out that they were a "brother" or a "sister," people would be killed in cold blood. Whether you stopped or not didn't seem to make much difference; it seemed to be just a matter of chance.

In front of the building there was already a crowd of people bursting with joy, and the marchers led by Umbellina immediately fixed their eyes on the burned-out shell of a *maximbombo* that had been hit by FAPLA fire. One of the *maximbombos* that the FNLA had tried unsuccessfully to use to win over the people of Luanda, offering them free transportation in those luxury buses sent in by the forces of imperialism. Only now this *maximbombo* had taken on the appearance of a dental plate pulled out of the mouth of a dead murderer. In and of itself it spoke volumes. Of how the people rejoiced at seeing the vehicle in this condition, completely burned, tireless, its fenders resting on the asphalt, with anything detachable on the inside immediately ripped out and carried off by those bold souls who climbed into it first. For here the removal and carrying away of trophies were still ongoing, women carrying sofas on their heads, stoves, chairs, machine chassis, gear wheels, all being hauled away as symbols of the victory over the oppressors. Victory over the nightmare.

"VICTORY! VICTORY!" It was Umbellina who led the chant. Up above, an MPLA flag, albeit small and discolored, waved proudly in the wind on the pole where, just a short time before, the yellow, white, and red puppet flag had hung. And the large letters "FNLA" had also been ripped down. All that remained was "People's House." "VICTORY! VICTORY!" they all shouted, clapping their hands.

Around the third corner on the left-hand side another demonstration as large as the one that had formed around Umbellina on Catete Street now appeared, to swell the celebration still further. They came on and on, in imposing numbers. But they suddenly stopped because there stood before them a cordon of *tuga* soldiers. They were challenged by the officer in command of the patrol. He was trying to persuade the demonstrators not to advance, but advance they did, with the fury of the shackles and dungeons of the past bursting apart. And, responding to the order words, with their hearts in their mouths, they broke through the cordon.

Then the demonstrators in Comrade Umbellina's battalion began responding to the order words coming from the other group and crowding forward to make those in front quicken the pace, all with the intent of reaching and joining these comrades who had defied the *tuga* army.

As the two masses were closing on each other, Umbellina recognized in the first ranks before her a very familiar profile.

Her legs almost gave way under her. Her eyes fixed themselves on that figure before her. No, it wasn't a dream! Inside, Umbellina was completely transformed, as she now really had to hunt for the most opportune things to say.

And if she pretended in the midst of this general rejoicing, and kept back the sad news?

While she labored amidst these doubts, her legs were still carrying her forward with greater energy, which rose to her lips in the form of "hooray, hooray," interspersed with sobbing and the free flow of tears. That is the way it was going to be!

"The struggle . . . "

"GOES ON!"

"Victory . . . "

"IS CERTAIN!"

The figure on which Umbellina's eyes were riveted was but a few steps away. Commanding the other group! With a fresh smile firmly fixed on her lips, Umbellina closed her eyes, clenched her teeth, and went forward with her hands held out toward that familiar face.

"Do you know, comrade? It's fate that it happened today. But Kito . . . "

"I know," she answered, in a tone of resignation. I've been to the morgue. But the FNLA is dead! Dead!" And saying that she grabbed Umbellina around the waist, raised her left fist in the air, and, the veins in her neck swelling, began to shout: "VICTORY! VICTORY! VICTORY!"

Umbellina had an attack of laughter. She snatched off her Afro wig, raised it high into the air, and chimed hoarsely, "THE M-P-L-A IS THE PEOPLE; THE PEOPLE ARE THE M-P-L-A," everyone clapping their hands and stomping their feet on the ground with all their might in response to the order words shouted out by Umbellina and Mimi, who, wrapped in each other's embrace, laughed, cried, and shouted with the satisfaction of two comrades who have found each other after a great many years of separation.

The people propose and the people dispose. They had been elected by the people.

They were two queens of Carnival!

Five Days after Independence

There were four of them in two ranks of two and the third rank had three because they were eight in all and with their commander out the formation was uneven.

Part One

And when the shells sowed a nervous confusion among the people and automatic weapons sang out in bursts and with louder volume their rhythm of death, the city would suddenly be transformed into a panic in which each resident's fear would reveal itself in either an instant of meditative silence or vocal outburst, frozen anticipation or physical flight.

Cars, trapped where they stood, would sound their horns impatiently. The red lights would have no effect whatsoever. Others, even driving down one-way streets, seeing an interminable line ahead, would turn around and go in the other direction illegally, madly racing to try to find another route that would get them to the safety of their homes or to a place where they could stay the night, the whole night through, awaiting further news about the fighting. Worse yet were the even greater number of people on foot! Precipitous departures from work, each person heading for his or her best and quickest route, they would run into one another, cross everywhere but in the cross-walks and in their haste walk in other illegal places, rip their plastic carrying sacks and even drop the sandals off their feet, so preoccupied were they with a single objective: not to lose any time. And even worse to see—if anyone had bothered to stop and look—was Catete Street. Because of the street's width, motorized vehicles could get up speed in their roaring flight while, on the sidewalks, the crowd ran along in fright, the people using the last moments of sun-light to make their way into the welcoming *bairros*. Oth-ers, calmer and better prepared, found time to visit the su-permarket and stock up on canned goods, because they knew from experience that when the war started up in Lu-anda no one could even guess when the cease-fire might come.

The central city was certainly the safest place to be, with the *tuga* forces patrolling in their pretense of neutral-ity; a person could usually find shelter in whatever build-ing was at hand and let the night fire transform itself into the light of day, reclaimed in its serenity. Even so, the work-ing-class people would leave it in droves. That's just how they are! Like a fish that knows instinctively the places where the waters flow slowly (but also where the invisible nets are plied), the people would leave the city asphalt and head to the *musseques,* places where the storm of bullets rained down the hardest. Because while they were the tar-get that FNLA hatred honed in on most, it was also from those staggered rows of dwellings and paths of contention, conspiracy and hidden weapons, that the popular resis-tance was primarily mounted. And we might note that this resistance was widespread long before our revolutionary vanguard (speaking through Agostinho Neto,* our comrade and, as such, more than our president) declared it official. It is for that very reason that, in homage, I bring this paragraph to an end before moving on in my telling of the events that took place.

In the process, that paragraph now finished, I must also note for all historians present and future that it was in the *musseques* beyond the asphalt of the city that the enemies of the people paid the most dearly. To be sure, it was there that they committed crimes without number. But in recompense they were felled like dumb birds on their way to plunder fruit, unaware that in that orchard that was not their own there were people who had sweated to plant the trees and were lying in wait to riddle trespassers' wings with well-aimed shot. And to go one step farther: the FNLA were little more than careless sparrows lured into the birdlime spread by the *pioneiros*.

So the people ran. They ran right to the *musseques*, to the places of past suffering. Places of endurance. Places of death as well, but always places of victory. It is certain! For the struggle goes on.

This, then, with nothing added and nothing deleted, is the way things happened.

There were four of them in two ranks of two and the third rank had three because they were eight in all and with their commander out the formation was uneven!

"March in place," the commander ordered. The *pioneiros* were going through their drills. This time they had commenced close-order drill in front of the COL,† across from the MPLA *Delegação*. The commander wore a black-

---

* MPLA leader and first president of the People's Republic of Angola.
† Another of the MPLA buildings in Vila Alice, acronym unclear.

73

and-white checkered net shirt that stretched tight across his chest every time he shouted out his commands of leadership, stomping the ground energetically with canvas boots, size forty-one, scavenged from what they were wont to call "the first great war" and made into a combat trophy (except that he had to be careful with his right foot because the boot on that side had a tear in the toe, which was held together by a cleverly tied nylon cord). And even with camouflage pants twice his size, which for that reason were rolled up and secured with cord on each leg, the diminutive comrade gave orders like a thirty-star general, duly honoring and paying homage to the *nom de guerre* chosen for him by his subordinates: "Kwenha."[*]

"Halt!" the commander ordered the instant the ambulance siren was heard.

All the people started running in the direction of the SAM. The vehicle came at full speed, the driver slammed on the brakes, and the ambulence skidded to a halt in front of the first-aid station.

"What do you think you're doing, comrades?" the *pioneiro* commander asked. But the words had no effect; they, too, took off, like a released spring, running to see what the ambulance's arrival portended. And Comrade Kwenha, deserted by his troops, bowed to majority will and raced along in their trail. Inside him, the same excitement felt by the scores of other onlookers who were spontaneously gathering about.

Then the vehicle wheeled around and you could hear the gears grinding. It moved in reverse toward the door.

Two FAPLAs rushed to pull open the back doors of the ambulance. The siren continued to wail, synchronized

[*] Like Gika and Valodia, an MPLA hero; the name is often rendered as "Kwenhe."

with the little red light blinking an on-and-off warning. Four nurses wearing smocks over their camouflage waited at the ready.

"Stand aside, comrades! Give me room! We can't work this way, comrades!"

The two soldiers tried to seal off the flanks with their weapons, but they just pretended to be ready to push the people back or to deal a blow to the standing order that the populace should suffer no maltreatment. And in any case they, too, spent most of the time with their eyes on the ambulance. Everyone wanted to see if whoever was inside was alive or dead.

"That's close enough, comrades," shouted the doctor, his arms in the air. "Don't you understand that we have to work quickly? If comrades come in on the verge of death, how can we hope to save them under these conditions? Are you MPLA comrades or aren't you?"

Access lanes opened. The noise subsided. But necks craned higher as a result.

The first victim to be brought out was an MPLA soldier. You could tell by his khaki shirt collar and his boots. The sheet he was wrapped in was soaked in blood, and it was still running red.

"He must be dead."

The doctor confirmed the supposition, nodding his head. And then the outcry began to intensify.

"Damned FNLA."

"I just want to know where they brought him in from."

"We have to run those murderers out of here."

"How can the comrades at the Palace even stand to be in a coalition government with those murderers?"

"Give us all weapons and the people will take care of them."

"Who's the dead man?"

"Comrade Nino."

Then, dragging her sandaled feet along the middle of the street, a woman broke down, wailing shrilly, and from the way she pulled her hair and the tears that flowed from her eyes, it was obvious that she was the victim's mother, a relative, or someone else close to him.

Next they put a man in his sixties on a stretcher.

"He caught a round in the leg," muttered one soldier, spitting fury.

Then they brought out a man who had been hit in the abdomen. He came with his wound unbandaged, blood running down his denim overalls. There were still old machine parts covered with grease hanging from one of his pockets. Everyone understood: a mechanic shot while he was on the job.

"Comrade Doctor, he's very badly hurt. I don't think he's going to make it," said one of the nurses.

The doctor shot back: "But why do they bring dead comrades and comrades in need of surgery here to us? We aren't a morgue or a hospital. I'm tired of saying it: under these conditions the best we can do is first aid and minor surgery. But they always just send them on to the SAM, a house converted into a do-everything station, and . . . "

"And what? Calm down, comrade; should we start plasma?"

"That's all we need! Here we have a doctor from the bleachers," someone joked scornfully.

" 'Calm down' is what I say! Come on, comrades, let's get these people back. We're in the middle of a war here, and it'd be a good idea to cut the *kazukuta*. I am the doctor here, no one else." And he beat his chest with a closed fist.

At that point the soldiers became more aggressive and forced the people to disperse.

The ambulance, which all the while hadn't shut off its motor or its siren, not even the blinking light on top, swung sharply to the right, and everyone got a look at the comrade with the beard who was driving and the two FAPLAs with him.

Afterward, a small gathering formed in front of the *Delegação,* and the *pioneiros* set themselves up there in their habitual intent of listening to the talk about the fighting. And the rumblings did soon begin. Some people wanted to know the exact time the firing started. Others were more concerned with where the first shot came from. Still others declaring, as though they had an understanding of such things, that the most important piece of information was whether the shelling that had ceased an hour before was FNLA or ours. If it was FNLA, you could expect there to be casualties, deaths, mourning. If it was ours, the puppets would have taken a big beating. And there were other people ready and willing to answer all such questions: locale, time. Some who had been witnesses "with these eyes that the earth will some day reclaim." Others had even helped with the recovery of the corpses. Even some who brought news about numbers: so many casualties for them, so many for us.

"Of course, but to my humble understanding we have to train our FAPLA comrades not to respond to provocation. Quite often, those miserable beings who go by the name of FNLA discharge one shot of provocation on the order of some Johnny or some Kabangu and then one of our comrades lets loose a whole volley in return, which leads to another and then yet another. And we all know what happens then. The people get killed. And the damage to our economy? Services brought to a halt, schools suspended. Only someone like myself who is involved with these questions because of his job can really understand all the ways that total breakdown is threatened as a result. Sometimes even through the fault of our own comrades. We have to change people's outlooks, calm them down so that some understanding can sink in." And he readjusted the knot of his tie.

"Shut up, comrade," advised a heavy woman in a worn black dress. "That's just more old official-sounding horseshit."

"But I have the right to make my opinion known, don't I? Your position is the reactionary one because it doesn't democratically allow others' opinions but instead advances superfluous and dismissive analyses."

"Me . . . reactionary? Just take off that colonial tie, you, you pretentious shithead!" And with those words she grabbed her interlocutor by the shoulders.

A small scuffle resulted. Comrade Stella and other *Delegação* workers who had come down from the first and second floors of the building tried to reestablish peace. Pulling on one's arm, pulling on the other's, she said that he said that she said, and the comrade in the black dress finally withdrew toward the corner of the COL, protesting all the while.

"Comrades, we're all on edge, but let's dump it all on the FNLA; it shouldn't be us against each other," was the advice of Comrade Osvaldo, head of the *Delegação* office.

The original theoretician nodded his head in agreement. He was a man with a lot of white in his hair and a paunch that bespoke the downing of more than his share in Sunday *funjadas.** And so thoroughly marked by colonialist practices in public service that he had not yet abandoned the habit of formal dress. He was completely undone, unable to decide what to do, first pulling his coat closed and then opening it up again, showing his party militant's card to some of the bystanders, ever afraid that in

---

* A meal featuring a popular dish of meat stew and cornmeal.

the midst of the crowd there could be someone who would toss out the unfair label of "provocateur" simply because of his manner of dress.

"Look here! This comrade was interned at São Nicolau!* Sometimes tongues start getting loose for no reason at all," added a *Delegação* employee, with the intent of assuaging the woman's fury.

"Oh. You mean they give out suits like that at São Nicolau? Then I think I'll go too."

Suddenly, however, everyone wheeled about and came to attention; not even the smallest throat-clearing was heard. In Vila Alice the lowering of the flag at the MPLA *Delegação* always paralyzed the road from one end to the other. It didn't matter how far people were from the flag, they got out of their cars, off their motorcycles, and, as a reflex action from seeing someone in front of them standing at attention, they formed a long chainlike line looking on in silent respect.

All it took, however, was the call of "Victory" from the soldiers of the guard, the final stomp of their feet, and their dismissal for the woman to start in fuming again. One soldier tried to put an end to the uproar. "You're just trying to make trouble, right comrade? What you need to do, auntie, is get to work, produce for the good of the cause."

"What do you mean 'make trouble'? You're nothing more than a child, even with that rifle. I'm looking for Comrade Lúcio. I'm here to tell him that my son was killed by the FNLA. I know what I'm doing. Why is it that it's the little people who keep getting killed? Is the MPLA the people and the people the MPLA or not? Then you have to

* A prison camp under Portuguese colonial rule.

give all the people guns. I've come here today, straight to the Hall of Delegates, to try and see Comrade Lúcio Lara."

"Down with the antirevolutionary *kazukuta*," said a young man with long hair.

"You're talking to me about antirevolutionary *kazukuta*, with that hair, bell-bottom pants, high-heel shoes like women wear? If you were my son, I'd show you *kazukuta*. I can't even tell for sure whether you're a man. Why aren't you in the FAPLA? What do you do anyhow, you bum?"

The laughing lasted but a brief moment. The more timid of the people raced off instinctively. The greater number regrouped in front of the *Delegação*. Some cars took off at high speed.

"That was close," one of the FAPLAs underscored. In fact, the two shell explosions had been very loud, and before the vestiges of the dispute could be rekindled, bursts of antiaircraft fire resounded, and then three more hits.

Comrade Stella put her hands to her head. "It's coming from Avenida Brasil. My daughter, eight months pregnant, is in the UNTA* building. Oh, my God!"

There were onlookers lying face down on the ground, staying close to the *Delegação* building, as they always did when the firing was heavy. FAPLA comrades were scurrying up and down the stairs, and from the COL there emerged two reconnaissance vehicles with soldiers in place, while others ran to reinforce positions on the nearby street corners. The firefight was increasing in intensity at a frightening rate.

A commander came to the door. "Please, comrades. I've got my orders. Move along! You're only in the way here."

* Another of the MPLA buildings in Vila Alice.

The employees hesitated for a moment, not knowing whether to go back into the building or not.

"I don't even want to think about my daughter," reiterated Comrade Stella. And the department head, stroking his thin moustache, pontificated in his nasal whine: "Comrade Stella, you always think disaster. C'mon!" And, turning his head almost automatically: "And you, *pioneiros?* Why are you still hanging around? Everyone else is leaving. Why not you? Aha! Because you don't have anything better to do, you don't go to school or anything. That's right, isn't it? A real *pioneiro* isn't a vagrant, you know. But you're here day in and day out wandering around the *Delegação*, your parents always having to come look for you. Is that a way to live your lives? Where do you get food to eat? Wherever you can? What are you doing here now? Get! Can't you hear the shooting?"

"But the fire is way up in the air; it isn't even hitting the tops of the buildings."

"Now look what we've come to. Even kids are tossing out opinions about the war. Get . . . now! A *pioneiro* has to act like one. And I don't want to see another one around here!"

The *pioneiros* could still hear Comrade Stella's last lamentations as Comrade Osvaldo ordered all the workers back to their jobs. Then they began an abashed march in the direction of the Empire movie theater.

Commander Kwenha was crestfallen, as though he were a general covered with decorations who had seen his commander's stars unjustly deprecated in public. But the decorations, the real ones, still remained inside his chest.

For the first time, the group had been chastised there. Right at the MPLA Hall of Delegates. And just because they were out on the streets, they had been called "vagrants." They did, after all, have five bases! They had participated, without taking a single casualty, in all the battles. They had recovered two FNLA weapons and had passed them on to the first FAPLA patrol that they came across. A truly marvelous squadron! One that, even before it had a name, had been present and had helped with the rooting out of the Chipenda followers. No, they couldn't give much credence to those empty words. And it was just high fire, no hits, just as they said it was. Which was why, while some bursts whistled high over João de Almeida Street and FAPLA comrades hunched down alongside walls, in doorways, and at street corners, their guns at the ready, the *pioneiros* just walked along, unhurriedly, meditating on their next operation.

The bursts of fire stopped. Then, immediately after the moment of silence, there was an exchange of four or five single shots. But they were off in the distance and sounded as though they were merely trying to deny the cessation of fighting.

"Comrades. Close formation!"

And the whole group scrambled to get into the customary arrangement: four in two ranks of two and the third rank with three because they were eight and with their commander out the formation was uneven.

"The firing seems to have stopped, but it's better to keep up reconnaissance."

The sun was just beginning to set. The *pioneiros* continued down João de Almeida Street. In front of the DIP* they crossed to the other side of the street so they could look at the "Wall Journal," stopping, fascinated, in front of the clippings showing a photo of Comrade President and *pioneiros* marching with their slingshot rifles. A ritual.

* The Department of Information and Publicity (Departamento de Informação e Propaganda), another of the MPLA buildings in Vila Alice.

Even though the postings hadn't been changed in days, they again engaged in the contemplation that was a part of the group's operating procedure. They drew their comprehension from the photographs; no one in the platoon knew how to read. They had at their disposal only the letters *V* and *C* drawn with the star, the symbol that they scratched in the sand in places where they went, always chanting, in a kind of magical ceremony, the words "Victory Is Certain."

"We ought to get going, comrades."

And the platoon set out again on its march, neither fast nor slow, paces measured through the experience of war.

At the end of the street, they entered the environs of the Empire theater. For the squadron, the movie theater was an obligatory patrol stop, even though on days of fighting the regularity with which it passed through this locale might be decreased. Not that some people could stand to let much time go by without returning to their customary landmarks. All it took was for the shooting to stop for two or three hours and they would venture out on crazy dashes on motorcycles or in cars, others on foot, just to get cigarettes. The bolder ones could even be seen getting together on street corners in calm discussion of the general situation, sometimes into the early hours of the morning. It's true: you can look it up in documents from the time when His Excellency the High Commissioner had proclamations promulgated over national radio in the name of the National Defense Commission, calling them "codes of law and sovereignty." But the more that peace and ceasefire were preached, the fewer chances people took. And if the proclamation said that people should be inside by such-and-such an hour, all the more were people to be seen out beyond that time. Not a single person took him seriously! Not even the reactionary Portuguese of that stripe who, after the carnations of April 25,* still dreamed of baptizing yet another piece of our land with the name of Freixo Sword-at-the-Belt (or at-the-flank)! No one took him seriously because:

First of all, His Excellency was more than a bit at odds with intelligence, the fact that he was an air-force general notwithstanding.

And, second, in a place as clothes-conscious as Luanda, he wore pants that were baggy in the seat but, in the style of fifteen years earlier, tapered at the leg, the whole affair ending in pointy-toed shoes, the kind used to squash cockroaches in room corners. He was what the collective sense of propriety might call a mannequin modeling sartorial mediocrity, 1940s colonial style. And there were those who claimed to know, through privileged information coming from His Excellency's very own domestic staff, that his underwear consisted of short, English-style underpants in a cut that the Athletic Club goalie of the 1950s would not even have wanted to use in workouts behind closed doors. That was the example we had to live with! And as far as headgear was concerned, we'd better drop the subject altogether.

However, in the third place, a certain leisure-time poet had written in his date book a capsule description of the general that circulated among some para-intellectual groups supportive of the Revolution, to wit: that the general had neither wings attached to his feet nor a propeller mounted on his head because:

Item four, he had proved the mineral scale incorrect by being harder to dent than a diamond. What's more, there's proof: one day, the people, banded together thousands

---

* The Portuguese revolution of April 25, 1974, was called "the Revolution of the Carnations."

strong, marched on the Palace. With signs, banners, and megaphones. Our leader withdrew to his air conditioning. The people started shouting, "Down with the High Commissioner!" This small fry then came to the balcony, with that face that only an addled painter might have chosen to render. And he smiled. The people began to fume: "Get the hell out of here!" About which he confessed to his closest collaborator—fittingly, a mush-mouthed colonel who stuttered—that this was his greatest political victory ever in these lands of Diogo Cão!

Now, my comrades. And ladies and gentlemen, too, since some of you haven't merited the intimate address of "comrade." Please pardon this interruption of our story, but the narrator of events is in fact trying to restrain himself, or else he would go on speaking of the general for as long as it takes to travel from Cabinda to Cunene. On foot! For many were the hours of pained exasperation during which I had to put up with the man. Be aware that it is only out of respect for his forebears that I resist reproducing his name in full. For the narrator of these spare, un-Nobel-aspiring lines was intimately acquainted with the general. If only he had had one scintilla of the brain function possessed by any one of the Young Pioneers, heroes of this piece of rambling prose—which, once it appears in print, I intend to send to the general with the dedication "Stand at attention! Because here in Angola there's writing going on!"

So that there can be told all the stories of all the youngsters who are forever going to walk tossed on the foam of that blue sea of ours. Of those youngsters with all our eyes on their eyes looking to the future like a horizon of certain victory. Of those youngsters who have marched under fire against fire. Of those youngsters, knowers of song, inventors of songs that were anti-imperialist marching orders. Of those youngsters drinking in tears our savoring of so overwhelming a joy whenever one more hectare of land in this country of ours was liberated. Of those youngsters like a primer of practical knowledge to which every one of the elders could turn in order to learn what he needed to teach those coming up behind him. Of those sea-youngsters. Of those do-it-all youngsters. Of those youngsters in front of the Empire movie theater posters looking only at the figures because they don't know how to read and, despite that, understanding important things like freedom. Of those youngsters who down on the avenue face the cars, the motorcycles roaring about in the uncertainty of a lull in the war, everybody running, volumes of people, *the* people, on foot. No one yet knowing if the firing is over or if it will start in again. And everybody heading for the *musseques*. The mothers. Mothers who can see in their mind's eye a son in the morgue at that very hour. Or a son missing. Mothers who had heard the stories of the recent past: anonymous cadavers piled high. There was no more room for them, no way to deal with the end of life or people to carry out the minimal task of preparing burials. Mothers horrified at hearing about corpses already infested with worms in the morgue. Those people, all those people, ran between volleys of bullets, just as bullets cut between hope and uncertainty. As they arrived at their destinations, "My God" was on the mothers' lips. The mothers of the people.

But at this moment there were no shots reverberating, and even if there had been, the Kwenha squadron was not under orders to take cover. They traversed the plaza. People passed, each one hurrying to get to his or her destination as quickly as possible, some defying the FAPLA patrols by choosing to use dangerous routes. The *pioneiros* scrutinized everything from top to bottom. Because that, too, was group operating procedure: when they found reason to be suspicious of anyone, they would hasten to the

comrades at the COL to report. But before that they would
ferret out that individual's route, where he or she lived,
name, relatives, associates. In effect, they wrote a mental
note to be kept with unerring precision in their voluminous
memory. Sometimes they would sit around categorizing:
"That guy must be a lackey; that one is a troublemaker . . . "

Lamps were being lit even though the vestiges of day-
light were still sliding away in the distance, on the seaside,
in flaming sunset tones. The *pioneiros* quit the plaza. Commander Kwenha headed his group as it patrolled the streets
of Vila Alice. Homes of MPLA people every one. Some of
them quiet. At the doors of others, talk going on about the
expectation of more shooting. And always tenderness and
love showing in the faces and in the questions that the
people asked from their doorways or from within their
yards. Almost anything one of the soldiers told them they
believed. How the war was going, how it wasn't, if they
could go out or not, and the FAPLA guarantee that the
FNLA would never come into Vila Alice because it was
impossible—that band of cowards, always shooting from a
distance or from ambush, catching solitary comrades off
guard, usually unarmed civilians, never engaging the
MPLA unless the FAPLA forces were numerically inferior.
"Imperialist lackeys!": that was the sacramental phrase.

One of those conversations was taking place in one
doorway now. The *pioneiros* paused to be able to hear the
gruesome details: "They go around in ambulances. The
comrades don't suspect an ambulance, and suddenly they
open fire."

"We have to get our hands on them," one woman,
leaning against the doorjamb, was saying.

"But they've already been caught." Some *pioneiros* no
bigger than those over there. The ambulance had been
stopped, and they had punctured its tires. Some of them
stayed around, talking to those guys, using terms like

"brother," while others ran to report. When the FAPLA got there, there were four Zaireens next to the vehicle. One of them opened fire. The *pioneiros* dived under the ambulance. Then the comrades answered the fire.

"And . . . ?" inquired the woman.

"Four to none. We had just one wounded."

"Four to none?"

"Yep. Four of them dead as doornails."

They had been forced to disband from around the *Delegação*, but by now all the dejection of that incident had dissipated. *Pioneiros* their own size, boys making weapons, catching FNLA soldiers, and even some Zaireens, the guys who speak French!

A solitary shot rang out, nearby, no more than two blocks off to the right. The soldier who was telling the news set his coffee cup on top of the wall, said good night, and took off like a shot, still chewing his sandwich.

"It's ours. It's a 'pepechá' automatic. It was a frightened comrade. Something moved, probably just a cat," explained Commander Kwenha to a group of wary bystanders.

They were unerring about such sounds. They could distinguish a bazooka from an automatic antiaircraft gun or an artillery piece. Only one thing gave them pause for fear: that was the mortar. Because it rose up out of the barrel, made a curve in the air, and could then drop randomly to earth and land unsuspected right where someone was. About all the others, they understood the minimum margin of safety.

"Hey, comrade! Come back afterward. Just ring the bell," said the woman, closing her door.

"Yes, comrade!" the soldier answered back, as he disappeared around the corner.

And the group, very much taken by this moment of relishing successes, also began its march again.

When they reached the crossing where the FAPLA had turned to the right, they paused, the commander hesitating.

"Straight ahead."

The shot heard earlier was not enough to command the *pioneiros'* attention. A patrol wagon passed. A FAPLA was manning his bazooka on top of the cab. At the end of the road, almost where Avenida Brasil started, you could see a long line of parked cars. That point marked the end of the area controlled by the FAPLA, and whoever wished to pass that line always took the diametrically opposite route to do so.

"*Pioneiro,* could you please help me here?" asked a young woman who was carrying wooden cases of beer into a yard.

The cases were stacked on the sidewalk. The *pioneiros* sprang to the task. When they went in with the beer they found themselves in a huge yard with a concrete slab floor and a wooden arbor above. In the middle was a table opened fully out, with a white cloth on top and loaded with food: meats, pastries, seafood, even bottles with silver paper covering their tops.

"So there really is food in Luanda," observed one of the youngsters as he struggled to lift one of the cases.

They made four trips. As they brought in their last load, they saw three men dressed in suits and ties, like the one who had gotten into the altercation in front of the *Delegação.* A fiftyish woman with cheeks caked with rice powder clapped her hands: "Let's go; there's no time to lose."

"I find it ironic, comrade. It's just our luck that the baptism would fall on a day when there's shooting."

Children dressed in Sunday clothes started filling the space around the squadron, fascinated with the slingshot rifles. The *pioneiros* just showed them off, not allowing the other children to touch. The times they lived in had impressed upon those children a precociousness in which they accepted war as a serious game of life and death.

One of the fancily decked-out men, apparently the owner of the house, took off his coat and hung it on a coat tree. His suspenders stretched tight over his huge belly, and the end of his tie—which was tied in the tiniest of knots—was tucked into a trouser waistband pulled up higher than his belly button. He clapped his hands, calling out: "Yes, let's go to it. But the first to go will be the *pioneiros*. This is, after all, a children's party." And picking up a plate with pieces of grilled chicken on it, he approached the youngsters.

People began to crowd around the tables. Three women hastily brought out the beer that had been kept on ice blocks in two halves of a metal drum. Someone started up the music. The woman of the house opened soft drinks for the children. And everyone started in eating and drinking, talking and laughing as though everything were going along wonderfully in their world.

It was a celebration like so many other parties and commemorations put on by the MPLA petite bourgeoisie. And, so as not to seem totally incongruous, the talk tended toward the topic of war events. The MPLA was like that: a wide front. People of diverse political backgrounds, various stripes, often steadfastly advocating their own particular position, contradictions that clearly bespoke each person's roots, but always all united in the ambitious notion of wiping out armored cars or even shooting down airplanes sent by the imperialists. The language was highly codified. "Imperialism," "neocolonialism," "puppets," "lackeys," "people power" were all terms that rolled off every tongue. Even the old women mixed them in with "God" and the saying of their rosaries. And the dances went on even on days when the shells flew. Only the music spoke for them of the Revolution and its heroes. The old habit of the good life went right on. A pretext could always be found! People would contradict themselves and in mid-celebration even suggest that the festivities should cease because they amounted to a form of corruption.

"What's all this church business if there won't be church anymore?"

"That's right! Especially since the settlers were the ones who introduced the 'J' word to begin with."

By now some were even beginning to question whether the baby should be baptized.

"It's just so as not to upset Grandma," argued the host, by way of justification.

"They talk and talk, but they know their way to where the party is. They're just talking to hear themselves talk," added the woman of the house.

And her husband went on: "What's more, the parents wanted it. They telephoned from Lisbon."

"C'mon. As a matter of fact, I never quite got this story about your son and his wife. Did they go to live up there in Tugaland or what?"

"Now look. She's undergoing medical treatment. Don't talk like that, not even as a joke."

"Hey. Didn't it used to be that the priest came to the baptism party and drank with the best of them?"

"He'll be here. He's waiting a half hour, and if there's no more shooting he'll be here."

"Are those bottles of champagne over there just for looks?" kidded another of the guests, his mouth stuffed with lobster salad.

"Aha, a volunteer! Since the comrade here is the first to speak up, he can be the first to uncork a bottle." And the host picked up a bottle and put it in his hands.

"Attention, comrades!" And hunched over, arms out-stretched, he held the bottle tightly in both hands. "Your attention please, comrades. There, on the coat tree, our host's jacket is Mr. Holden Roberto.* I'm going to hit him square on. A bazooka strike right on the head of that sissy from Zaire."

And he unwrapped the tinfoil and began to twist the cork loose, carefully. "Here she goes!"

"Turn off the record player," a woman shouted. And at the very instant the music stopped, the revelers suddenly all raced frantically into the house, and the yard lights went out as though by magic.

Everyone piled into the living room, the bedrooms, and the bathrooms.

The *pioneiros* were left alone in the yard. This time even they had hunkered down and huddled up against the wall, because the volleys were very close by and the bullets were whining right over the top of the arbor.

"Turn out the lights!" And one by one the rooms were plunged into darkness.

"Comrade Elias, you doused me with champagne all over," complained the host, his head stuck under a sofa.

"I'm never in my life going to drink any champagne he opens. It's bad luck," commented a female voice.

"But I wasn't just talking. I scored a direct hit!"

"Now those guys have come into Vila Alice?"

"Yeah. That's the last straw. But while there are men like me who can shoot straight, they'll only come in here as prisoners. Anybody want some champagne? A good soldier is never separated from his weapon." And some people were still able to manage a good laugh.

"The damned holy man must have known. I had it

---

* Roberto was the leader of the FNLA; an Angolan by birth, he spent most of his young life in French-speaking Zaire.

smelled out, what with the priest staying away from the celebration . . .''

"Maybe the guy is even tipped off. Which one is he?"

"The priest from the Catholic radio station."

"You could have told me. Damn it! In these times that minister of God on earth is in the service of the devil, who's ordering up all of this."

"Whoa! You talk like you used to be in a seminary!"

The nearby weapon fire was interrupted by two almost simultaneous shell explosions farther away. Then there was another one close at hand, and the fire began to whine again. The *pioneiros* glimpsed the glare from some tracers cutting across the black expanse of the sky.

"But that fire is ours. It's from an AK-47." And saying that, Kwenha raced toward the gate with his companions in his wake.

He pressed the lever but couldn't get the gate to open. Locked. Then he twisted around in the net he was caught in, jumped up and balanced atop the wall on one foot, and dropped into the street. The others followed his lead with the euphoria of people who had regained their freedom.

The street was deserted. Just the *pioneiros*. Moving along bent over, using the protection afforded by yard walls and the sides of buildings. For them there could be only one objective: the place the shooting was coming from. They made a short sprint to cross an intersection. Out of the darkness at the corner there emerged a shape, revealing itself in the moonlight.

"Hey, *pioneiros*. Be careful, things are heating up."

"Yes, comrade," answered the last one in the line.

Heating up indeed. Volleys and explosions consecutively. Tracers slicing across the sky.

"It's Avenida Brasil!" shouted the commander. "We'll have to get there fast, to carry out reconnaissance."

They angled to the right at a steady run. They were taking the strategic route for situations such as this: go out of Vila Alice and up to the gravel road that runs on this side of the Cidadela. Then, depending on the intensity of the fire, take the paths most propitious for their objectives: to spy on FNLA movements on the Avenida Brasil while avoiding confrontation with any of the lackeys. Sometimes they covered dozens of kilometers. Hours and hours experiencing the most diverse of situations. Taking refuge in yards or comrades' houses, helping the FAPLA in small operations of opportunity, or pausing to study carefully the causes of this or that event. And if they saw that the puppet forces were planning a flanking move, they would run to give information about where the enemy soldiers were and how they were deployed.

On this occasion, it wasn't just the large amount of fire from Avenida Brasil that caught their notice, it was that most of the explosions were going off in a straight line along that thoroughfare, almost up to the Marçal.

"That's where Pedro Benge was killed," recalled the commander. "We have to find out where they are. Today the firing is all turned around."

They decided to adopt a waiting tactic, sighting in carefully on the buildings on the left-hand side, with the goal of trying to get a better sense of the lay of the land.

"Are you going to spend the night here, or what?"

They wheeled around. The words had come up from the trench a few meters to their right.

"We're on our way home," Kwenha answered.

"Where's home?" insisted the FAPLA, now on foot outside the trench.

Collectively, the *pioneiros* gave a deep sigh of relief. Some soldiers in the forward lines in relation to the Avenida Brasil were of course in the area. The squadron was aware of that. But so absorbed were they in unraveling the puzzle of the shooting as they moved forward that for a moment they had forgotten.

The FAPLA moved over next to them.

"Where's home?" he asked again, profiling a smile full of affection for the small adventurers who considered themselves great combatants.

"Home is in the Marçal, comrade."

"Hmm. Now listen. With that gun you'll have to be careful if you're caught. So be quick. The fighting in the Marçal is pretty heavy."

"Yes, comrade."

And, atop a wooden deck over a crater at the street's edge, they began to run.

It took only an instant for them to devour the remaining space and get to the edge of Avenida Brasil, the glorious objective of their efforts, the terrain that the enemy considered his. They knew it with their eyes closed, just as they knew almost all the roadways and alleys of the *musseques* that filled the world in which they played out their fantasies and which they now drew upon in war to exercise that mixture of astuteness and courage necessary to pursuit of the enemy.

Kwenha was panting with exhaustion. He pulled his shirt off, rolled it up, and stuck it in the oversized pocket in his camouflage pants. That was standard procedure. Near puppet territory, obscure the target, white-and-black checks.

Then they sat down in a circle with the commander in the middle. By a happy coincidence, the shots ceased and the squadron enjoyed a respite in that interval of silence in which the simple barking of dogs, a shout, or the roar of a motor inflamed the people's dubiousness as they thought about the contrast between war and peace. Because the shooting normally began at dusk, built in intensity, underwent its anguishing lulls, and by the time night was full grew in the hearts and thoughts of the people like a whirl-wind of fury. Shells could hit anywhere. Just who was daring to go out in those cars that from time to time came speeding down the asphalt?

"Hey, listen. An ambulance," observed one of the group, getting up on his knees.

They all turned their ears in the direction of the siren's wail.

"Down!" ordered the commander.

The siren's wail drew closer. All in a line, hugging the ground, hidden from view by a pile of old tires from the abandoned garage.

The ambulance passed by. Then a station wagon, also white.

"It's coming from the university hospital," judged Kwenha.

They were afoot for only a moment, following the ambulance's trail with their eyes and ears, failing to notice another vehicle coming in the same direction.

"*Tuga* troops," observed the commander. "Carrying sick people." Again on their feet, eyes fixed straight ahead, the red of the stop signs, the ambulance and the station wagon, now stopped. Then the Portuguese army Unimog also stopped in the same place.

The *pioneiros* knew: just a little up ahead the puppets were in control of the transit routes. The route to the university hospital. The route normally taken by nurses, doctors, personnel on duty, all MPLA people who had no choice but to travel through that zone so overflowing with lackeys. And they knew well the health service comrades' courage, because the squadron regularly patrolled the hospital environs, going inside, walking through wards, eating with doctors. And they also knew that the FNLA had put up a base right across from the hospital.

"Today the checkpoint is very close!"

The entire group seconded the commander's alarm. They had to alert the comrades immediately: there was an FNLA checkpoint nearby. That is why people who worked at the hospital were disappearing. Comrades who barely paid attention to the changes from night to day, going back and forth from the hospital to the SAM, from the SAM to the theater of battle or to the morgue. And in the memory of these little soldiers were revived images of the shelling of the hospital, the platoon inside, going about all night long seeing to the well-being of kids who had been removed from an infirmary located right on the fringe of the puppets' base camp, the shell blasting through the wall, the patients' panic, and, when the members of the government arrived, the personnel demonstrating with the dead bodies of victimized colleagues, the corridor drenched in blood, the repeated collective call: "Vengeance!"

Up ahead the three vehicles recommenced their progress. Kwenha gave a signal. They had to go notify the comrades! A quick dash through the dim lamplight and the group was on the other side of the avenue in a darker stretch, chosen for its small mango tree, under which they could design a plan for getting into the hospital. But then, all of a sudden, they had to dive to the ground, a nearby outburst, a chorus of shots with the addition of a heavier, rattling fire.

"Antiaircraft," one of the *pioneiros* specified, in a low voice.

The sound descended from above, and the squadron knew well the chronicle of that weapon set up on top of the FNLA's so-called People's House, which many soldiers had vowed to put out of commission.

They stood up, even though the firing went on. It was just the surprise that had made them drop to the ground, because for them gunfire was no big deal. Now the explosions took on a synchronized rhythm; the *pioneiros* counted it out, "One, two, *three!*" not even hearing the gun's whistle but detecting—and quite easily—the locations of the louder reports.

"The UNTA building, comrades!" shouted the commander, in a breach of the silence that the degree of danger dictated. "We have to reconnoiter the field and advance to the hospital. Onward, FAPLAs."

"*Pioneiros*," corrected one of his subordinates.

"*Pioneiros* or FAPLAs, it's all the same. It's the people. It's the M-P-L-A."

"Yes, comrade," the other agreed.

"We criticize you," declared another, his finger in the air.

"Yes, comrade; and I shall engage in self-criticism."

"Stop the talk. Do you hear?" Another outburst resounded in front of them. "I'm the commander; you chose me for the job."

And the platoon quickened its pace along the dark, curving roads that they knew inside and out. A garbage heap where cans were piled that might make a noise; they walked around it. When the moon lit up a clear spot in front of them that might reveal shapes, they slid around the edges. Even though they didn't know how to read, they had deciphered the MPLA order words by the shape of the letters. If, on a yard wall the shapes suggested opposition, they would go around.

"Onward!"

The *pioneiros* ran rapidly on in an advance that no one could have followed. No one could hear these masters of the night, for no one knew as well as they did the nights of battle, communed with those nights in clandestine security, heard their pained complaints, the barking of the dogs, the wailing of the ambulances, or contemplated the brilliant glow of their stars. And in that walk through such nights, they also disseminated the certainty of victory, somehow suspended between reality and imagination, dream, the words of Comrade President, the revolutionary chants, the demonstrations, and the dead of this present moment in Luanda, many of whom they found, unburied bodies, rotting in a pigsty of abandonment. Night paths.

"Onward! They're shelling the UNTA!"

The building in sight, the area the howitzers were honing in their crashing roar upon, causing windowpanes to rattle in the workers' hall, the working class, tools symbolically clutched in muscular hands, pleaded for them to scale the Palace stairs and on the balcony to grab the microphone in their hands in front of the vanquished FNLA High Commissioner and roar out unabashedly, at the top of their lungs: "Down with the lackeys of imperialism," the crowd responding with a force that could throw waves against the opposite shore of the ocean: "Down with them!" the entire working-class population, militiamen, OMAs, *pioneiros*, MPLA flags fully unfurled, the people in the midst of the people against the imperialists, the Kwenha squadron.

"Onward, comrades! We have to get inside!"

Just as the *pioneiros* made up their minds to go in, an even heavier barrage hit the building. Soldiers bounded down the back stairs, out the door, and immediately hit the ground. Others disappeared into the night.

Meanwhile, in the midst of the whining ricochets and the shattering of glass, the *pioneiros* heard shouting upstairs, the noise of the people in a panic, racing pell-mell down the stairs to flee out the front door the *pioneiros* went in two FAPLAs with guns in their hands protecting the staff's exit in a panic it seemed like the lackeys were firing point blank, and taking comrades by the hand and out the back the volleys came from up close two FAPLAs also coming down the stairs, four steps at a time, the squadron now on the first floor one soldier even calling out, to no avail, "Get out, *pioneiro,*" they got down the corridor, "onward, *pioneiros*" — the steps of boots lots of boots and a strange tongue that they didn't understand all the time the shouts getting louder all the time closer the *pioneiros* in the confusion of trying to find the back staircase and in that moment in which everyone tried to find the right way out the last of the *pioneiros* darted into a hall that he thought led in the right direction.

She was tightly clutching her belly. Frightened, she found her hands were the only weapons at her disposal to defend what she bore in her womb. They had crawled some seven or eight meters along the drainpipe when the *pioneiro* said "Here." And during all the time consumed in hearing the lackey voices so close by, the screams of the cook as she was being violated, then the lightning steps of the *pioneiro* as he stepped into the office and immediately peeked behind the curtains, through all that time up to this breathless moment, Carlotta still hadn't made up her mind if her life was saved or if this was just the drawn-out beginning of her death, her body still shaking inside her loose-fitting dress soaked through with sweat. At first she could see almost nothing. Then, in a terror that kept her from even blinking, she became aware of the aid provided by a strip of moon sliding down the mouth of the pipe, and her eyes began to explore carefully the inside of the drain, the *pioneiro,* his size, the slingshot rifle clutched in his hands, the youngster's dancing eyes and the tepid breath exuding from his mouth the fatigue of an experienced, mature guerrilla.

The *pioneiro* shifted his gaze back and forth, first to the end of the pipe and then to the young woman's dark silhouette, and when his ears were convinced that the bombardment had stopped, he took stock of his companion in the brief moment that was all that was necessary for someone accustomed to seeing in the dark.

"Is everything all right?"

"Yes, comrade," the young woman answered. "But what isn't is what's going on out there."

"That will be all right too. They'll be coming."

"Who?"

"My commander and the other comrades. Victory is certain."

She thrust her body forward the distance of half a meter in order to be able to put her right hand on the *pioneiro*'s face, the laugh of joy echoing in the depths of the pipe, the other hand over her mouth salty with tears.

"It has to be certain, *pioneiro*."

The youngster stretched out his upper body in meditative contemplation of the route of this pipe off into the mysterious darkness, a darkness into which the enemy would not dare venture. Then he turned his head back to the entrance. Carlotta stared at him. They could now see each other clearly, through a kind of subterranean moonlight.

"It has stopped."

"Yes. But it can start again. Vigilance!" And he pointed toward the opening with his slingshot rifle.

Carlotta took up her initial position again, hands on her belly, head inclined, looking right at the *pioneiro*, who kept his eyes riveted on the light at the opening.

"What is it?"

"Nothing."

His thoughts were like a statue contemplating itself in a mirror: the comrades must have got just about to the end of the corridor at the moment when the woman screamed and he found this young woman behind the curtains. They must certainly have then either retreated or else put on a feint right in the puppets' faces and found another stairway went down crept along slowly until they made it out into the dark. Now they are back together. One missing. Kwenha outlines a plan to find him. His miniature rifle stock banged against the inside of the pipe. The noise set up an echo. He concentrated harder. Or maybe: the comrades had hidden behind a curtain like the one in that room, Kwenha spying out through a hole he had made in it with his teeth. He had seen a whole band of puppet soldiers, the kind of weapons they're carrying, and he will never, ever forget the features of any one of them. A lackey pulling the hair of the woman comrade who screamed, another ripping up political posters, another smashing typewriters, still another breaking into the cash box. The comrades perfectly silent, no movement. Then the lackeys pull the woman, screaming, down the stairs. The comrades stay inside the UNTA building. But one is missing! Now the reconnaissance begins! Onward, FAPLAs!

"Open fire on them, comrades. Not an inch of ground to the enemy!"

The young woman, startled, removed her hands from her belly.

"What, *pioneiro?*"

"Nothing. Just thinking."

"But, are there people?"

"They'll be here."

"But who?"

"My comrades."

They felt a vibration coming from above the drain pipe and the muffled rumble of roaring motors.

"They'll pass," explained the *pioneiro,* eyeing the roof of the pipe.

The shaking continued. Carlotta also engrossed in the sensation of car after car passing over the hiding place.

"There are so many of them."

102

"It's a column," replied the boy. "Either *tuga* or lackey," he added.

"How can you tell?"

"We don't move that way, with so many vehicles in a line."

"And that gun, what can you kill with it?"

"Anything," answered the youngster, holding the weapon securely in both hands. "Imperialist lackeys."

"And what if there were an armored car?"

"I'd crawl inside and blow up the operator. Armor doesn't work without people. Once during a political rally, there was a comrade who spoke, saying that it's the man who makes the machine go."

"And if it's a ship?"

"What kind of ship?"

"A battleship?"

"We're not on the ocean here. But together my squadron will sink it."

"But have you ever sunk one?"

"No. Because the enemy doesn't come by sea. Besides, all the fisherfolk are organized by the MPLA. If they come, we'll sink them."

"And if it's a plane?"

"I'll shoot it down. Just let it fly low enough. A comrade told me about how he shot down a 'copter during the first one."

"During the 'first' what?"

"The first war of liberation."

"You think those are lackey cars."

"Yes, comrade."

The woman raised her trembling arms, flattening her hands against the top of the pipe. Slowly, in a gesture that approached that of prayer and emulation, she rubbed the palms of her hands against the corrugated surface. Her heart beat rapidly as she breathed the same fear and the same terror as when, after the bombardment, she had heard the FNLA boots scraping along the corridor at the UNTA installation, the words uttered in French, and Dina the cook screaming. The fear was being reborn in her.

"What if they stop right here close to us?"

"There's no danger down here. This is a liberated area. Base number five, Kwenha squadron."

"Keep your voice down!"

"Yes, comrade. But there's no way the enemy can know we're down here."

The way he caressed the barrel of the miniature rifle, its stock resting on the bottom of the pipe. Untouchable. Exuding not only confidence but also a sense of responsibility and an astuteness equal to the situation.

Carlotta lowered her arms to her belly, staring at the child with less and less worry about what events might bring. She wanted to ask about things, lots of things, to see if the *pioneiro* was sure of everything he said, that they would be here only another hour, that his guerrilla comrades would come to their rescue by then because the puppet forces would be dislodged from the building that stood but a couple of paces from the mouth of the pipe. But she didn't speak; she just looked the child over, as though she were in the presence of a hero who could know only victory.

The noise of the motors and the shaking of the earth could no longer be heard. What filled Carlotta's ears now was silence. Silence like blades of anguish within her anticipation. She fixed her eyes on the entrance to their hiding place. That's where they had entered, and it was the only way out. And close by, very close by, the puppet soldiers were doubtless rifling through UNTA documents and might think to go over the building grounds, the drainpipe. This drainpipe! She tried to penetrate the pipe's dense, endless blackness through swollen eyes. Where did this pipe start? Anyhow, if they got suspicious, they'd come to the entrance and there would be no rescue. Run, shout, call for help? How could they? And what good would any of it do? Was that a burst of gunfire?

And she broke down sobbing convulsively, her hands open over her face, her mouth half-closed so she wouldn't cry out loud.

Lizards, of many colors. With claws dug into the pipe's surface and eyes shooting sparks that lit up their thick, repugnant, fanlike scales. She remained motionless, terrified, hands pressed against her belly. Beside her the boy, fallen, dead, with his face unrecognizable, covered with blood. Hails of bullets rained down from the entrance. Suddenly, a flash of fire, a bluish lizard opening its mouth and flicking out its long red tongue. The lizard licking Carlotta's hair. And her wanting to turn her head away, being unable to . . .

The *pioneiro* shook her: "Wake up, comrade. We have to remain vigilant."

She opened her eyes with a start. And clenched her fists: "My God!" And with her memory still anchored in that recent brief nightmare she began to sob and to utter words incoherently.

The child inched a step closer, kept his left hand resolutely on his rifle, and with the other caressed her wet face.

"What's the matter? We're at war, and victory is certain. Nobody should cry. What if Comrade President knew a comrade was crying like this? You can't."

With tear after tear still running down her cheeks, she held back her sobs, lowered her head softly, and shamefully covered her face with the hem of her dress. The *pioneiro* was right. She was, after all, an MPLA militant. She shouldn't be crying.

Consoled by that sense of strength and of victory that Comrade Neto signified, she felt in her veins the warmth of hope, cemented by the vivid memory of the happiest and most joyful moments experienced in MPLA demonstrations and rallies, *pioneiros* raising dust by marching better than anyone else ever, people beyond number running toward the Palace in what was the Grand May Day parade. She rekindled her conviction of invincibility, in a kind of faith. It was just that, because she felt ashamed, she hid her face in the gathered hem of her dress. Even so, she took up her questioning of the *pioneiro* again.

"The FNLA won't get in here?"

"They won't."

"But they're right there in the UNTA. They might even have seen us come in. It's very near," and she pointed to the entrance to the pipe.

"They can't get in here," answered the *pioneiro*.

"Why not?"

The youngster drew himself together and rubbed his head with the entire set of fingers on his right hand, keeping his left wrapped firmly around the gun.

"This is one of the Kwenha squadron's bases."

"What squadron?"

"Our squadron; we call our leader Kwenha."

"A *pioneiro* squadron?"

"Yes, comrade. A squadron of fighters."

Raising her head, she became pensive, her eyes, filled with tenderness, rested on the *pioneiro*'s rifle and, in a gesture of modesty, she pulled her dress hem back down to cover her legs.

The youngster's assurances gave her confidence as she recalled, one after another, all the tales of heroism she had heard about *pioneiros*. Some who had forced the puppet soldiers out of their base in the Bairro Operário, others who had disarmed and hog-tied four soldiers from the invading Zairian army, and still many others who had time and time again guided the FAPLA in the discovery and capture of the lackeys.

She thought about the possibility of getting out safe and sound and felt a singular pride in being here, with a *pioneiro,* at this moment of danger and of war.

"Then, if this is your base, the other *pioneiros* can get in?"

"Yes, comrade."

"But then *they* could too."

"Who?"

"The FNLA." She lowered her voice as she uttered the word.

"Nah. Only the Kwenha squadron has the key to this base. And even if they did find us they'd be afraid to come in. You see, comrade"—and he pointed the little rifle toward the entrance—"only one person can get in at a time. And if I wipe out the first one, there's going to be a noise like cannon fire."

"What?" asked Carlotta, unable to mask her astonishment.

"The echo down here is very loud. Then their hearts will skip a few beats and nobody else will dare stick a nose in. But if they do, I'll wipe out another one. What's more, when Kwenha hears the echo, he'll know what it is and bring reinforcements."

Carlotta grew somewhat calmer and, as though having hit on the quickest way to get herself out of this prison, concluded: "But what if you just shoot now?"

"It'd be too soon. The enemy has only been here for a short time. They're hunting around. And also we could cross fire with our other comrades. Now is a time for calm."

Carlotta rubbed her hands together. She relaxed her body to adapt better to the uncomfortable shape of the pipe. She breathed in and out with more control, looking into the eyes of the *pioneiro,* who, out of the corner of his eye, was studying with some amazement the size of her pregnant belly. They were eyes glowing out from a face outlined by the head's bony structure, from which large ears protruded. She could see better all the time in this dim, humid hole from which now for the first time her nose picked up the putrid stench. It made her nauseated. She thought she was going to vomit, but, with the *pioneiro* there, she steeled herself against the shame that would come with breaking down again. She rubbed her hands together a second time. She needed something. That's it, a cigarette. The *pioneiro* would certainly not allow her to smoke down here, but nonetheless she had made a grave error in not grabbing her handbag when she hid behind the curtains. Then she imagined the puppet soldiers examining the picture on her militant's card, seeing her name, for they made a detailed list of MPLA militants marked for elimi-nation. And she squeezed her hands together angrily until a knuckle cracked. An even more foolish mistake had to do with her silly habit of carrying her watch in her purse and taking it out only when she wanted to know what time it was. Her mother had been right to berate her with "I bought you that watch so you could wear it on your wrist." And she had been proved right.

"What time is it, *pioneiro?*"

"Around nine," the youngster replied, closing his eyes and estimating.

"That early still?"

"Yes, comrade. In war, time moves very slowly; and things are only going to heat up more after midnight."

"Why?"

"Now is when our comrades will be preparing their operation."

"What comrades?"

"The FAPLA comrades. They'll come out of Vila Alice. First they'll meet, receive their instructions. A slow, cautious reconnaissance, then they'll advance and suddenly open fire on the enemy."

He spoke with a contagious optimism that caught Carlotta up as well.

What the *pioneiro* said rang true. She had spent many nights in Vila Alice. Going all night without sleep, helping where she could, sometimes right in the SAM when many wounded were brought in. And she had witnessed the departure of small groups of soldiers on their way to defend the people with no assurance of coming back alive. But they always set out holding their fingers up in a V for "Victory." And at dawn the news of the outcome would begin to filter in: prisoners, captured arms, ambulances racing back and forth to transport the wounded and dead. And, sure as sure could be, for every setback inflicted by the FAPLA the lackeys would take vengeance upon the unarmed populace, people telling of how they would come into a neighborhood, gather everyone together by force, shouting "Now is the MPLA the people, or isn't it?" and then blast away. Victorious guerrillas — in Vila Alice! And the *pioneiro*'s presence made her recall all those scenes. As a result, she felt stronger and bolder. One night could be got through; it would pass quickly. The child was certain that after midnight things would heat up again and then the FAPLA would retake this position, and she and the *pioneiro* would finally be able to leave their hiding place.

"Comrade . . . " Carlotta was startled out of her reverie. "How did they get into the building?"

"Who?"

"The FNLA," concluded the child, with the air of someone who had been meditating on the question.

"I don't know. The firing had been going on for more than an hour. No one worried much, since it was hardly the first time. The shells usually just whistle overhead and fall behind us, quite some distance away. At first tonight it was just the same as usual, mortar rounds but no real danger. But as it started growing dark, my God! Mortar rounds right on. Some exploded against the walls. And . . . "

"How's that?" asked the *pioneiro*.

"Yes, comrade! I heard sections of the wall fall and windows shatter."

"But that wall wouldn't go down from mortar fire coming from there."

"From where?"

"From Avenida Brasil. The fire falling here comes from there." The boy nodded his head as a sign of conviction.

"But glass broke. I heard it break."

"Then . . . the glass must have shattered from the reverberations."

"From the what?"

"It happens. The noise made by a mortar round when it lands is enough to shatter glass close by."

They were now looking at each other face to face, no longer glancing out of the corners of their eyes at the pipe opening. And little by little Carlotta got control of herself, forgetting her fear, the heavy, sinister atmosphere of the drainpipe, caught up as she was in the *pioneiro*'s knowledge.

"Then when did they come in?"

"I'm not exactly sure. The mortar fire kept on landing close. And then that heavy gun that you can hear even in Vila Alice started in."

"That's the 'Breda.' It's on their building on Avenida Brasil."

"Then we heard footsteps on the stairway, and that's when I hid behind the curtains. And what about you?"

"We came through on patrol. The Kwenha squadron."

And they stopped for a moment, looking at each other, perplexed, reliving the curtain, the stairwell, their flight. Then the youngster suddenly turned his head toward the depths of the pipe; the young woman did the same, horrified. Two eyes shone brightly in the darkness and were coming closer. Carlotta pulled up her dress, covered her face, thought for a brief moment about the possible discharge of the *pioneiro's* weapon, felt something move up next to her, bit down on her hem, and, through clenched teeth, uttered, "Help!"

Tears rolled thick down her cheeks but, caught up in the youngster's laughter, she broke out laughing as well.

"Shh, comrade. We're making a lot of noise," the *pioneiro* criticized, coming back to reality. "We *are* at war."

"But . . . whose dog is this?"

"The people's. He's the watchdog at base number five, Kwenha squadron, the terror of imperialism. Bazooka!" The dog rolled over and stretched out with an air of familiarity, nose sticking straight up, while the child scratched its belly.

"But where was he?"

"Close by."

"Doing what?"

"His job is to guard the base whenever he wants," laughed the *pioneiro*, patting the dog's belly while it opened its mouth and drew in its legs with sensuous pleasure.

Carlotta pulled herself a little bit forward and reached out her right hand. The dog growled.

"It's OK. You can pet him, comrade."

She shivered and tried to get control of her fear by pretending to play with the dog too.

The moonlight filtered in more softly now, toning the pipe's dull darkness with silver and outlining the three silhouettes.

Carlotta, less fearful, had adapted to the absence of light and was running her hands over the ears of the gaunt dog. Lying between the two people, it served as an extraordinary companion of faith dissipating the sense of isolation and of fear. The boy's face took on an aspect of affection and happiness as he watched Bazooka gradually give himself over to the young woman's touch.

The dog picked himself up, stretched, shook, and moved unconcernedly toward the pipe opening.

Carlotta and the *pioneiro* followed the dog's exit with their eyes. When it finally got out of the pipe and into the moonbeams' full smile, Carlotta returned to her absorption in the presence of this *pioneiro* so in control of himself as he adjusted his camouflage cap. And she spent some moments meditating on life coming, as it did, in conjunction with this war.

She still didn't even know the youngster's name. Two or three years before, people would always ask each other's names. Now everything was different. "*Pioneiro*" was enough. "Comrade," yes. But the boy had a name. And surely a family too. Nevertheless, Carlotta could see in the *pioneiro* the whole trajectory of the second war of liberation. People running through the streets of Luanda without fear of puppet fire, people with arms spread open asking for weapons, the multitudes shouting against imperialism. What was most contagious was the confidence in victory, the way the people organized with thought to the future, to independence. The way people persisted in the conviction that the "transition government" could lead to one outcome and only one: the MPLA in power and the lackeys defeated. Every day corpses turned up. Women were violated by ELNA soldiers. On the radio program "Angola at

War" the people came forward to bear witness. There were people who came in from the Uíge, or Malanje, or Lubango to tell how a husband was drawn and quartered before his wife's eyes, or a child was stabbed for speaking about the MPLA, or a girl raped by ten ELNA soldiers who then shaved her head with their swords and made her eat the hair. But none of those things intimidated the people. On "Angola at War" the announcers persisted with their message. Days thick with arms fire, everyone staying under cover and still tuning in the radio to the MPLA program, the order words, the beautiful hymns of the revolution. And, day after day, more revolutionary songs speaking of a fallen hero but always from within the certainty of victory. And on the days the puppets' talons closed most tightly around the popular resistance, the announcer's voice became even more forceful in proclaiming "Angola at War." And the next day, early in the morning of dew and quickened hope, the radio program would loose its antidote of humor upon the lackeys: Roberto, Savimbi, or Chipenda, imperialist pawns meticulously satirized for the people to hear.

Carlotta, with her fear forgotten. The *pioneiro*'s company, a flood of recollections, the day the *Delegação* arrived, the knot of humanity at the airport. As though she had not been quaking in terror only a little while before, almost tasting death, the sound of the combat boots, the cook's screams, the constant hammering of the fire, the shell explosions. Now with eyes wide open hands protecting her belly, she sees through her sleepless vigil half-dream half-nightmare the arrival of Comrade President, the fourth of February, first celebrated in Luanda with order words, flags, and songs. Carlotta right in the middle of the crowd. The word *comrade* beating impetuously against the shackled walls of the past, and always, always, the *pioneiros* marching—before every victory. After every victory.

Pioneiros marching after every setback. *Pioneiros* dying amid the firing just as the principle of life was being proclaimed in the coming independence. *Pioneiros* making weapons. *Pioneiros* attending the people's funerals, with sure step, natural gait, foot balanced in front, arm outstretched dancing in the future, head turned to the side, a song on their lips, the music of past suffering and, even stronger, the shout of the shouted prophecy: "The struggle goes on! Victory is certain!" Rifle butt resting on the ground, knees together, the big boots, the legs inside the long pants. The characteristic cap. Eyes shining two sentinels of hope. Carlotta looking at the *pioneiro* wide awake as she struggles not to let her head fall under sleep's assault but vigilance forces her to concentrate on remaining awake. Inside this drainpipe. Right beside the FNLA, who have occupied the UNTA building, because there is nothing more to talk to the *pioneiro* about. Just the weight of her body the whirlwind of thoughts in her head thinking the best still laughing inside at what had happened before in the UNTA building office now with her hands over her pregnant belly and the overwhelming sensation of having life. Seeing in the dark. Knowing that the opening was close by, through which came beams of light. Smelling the body sweat the dull putrid odor permeating the air in the pipe. Still hearing little sounds, lizards, rats in their normal routines of nighttime living. And maybe snakes. Carlotta had always considered snakes something from another world. That is how they can slide slowly over the ground and no one can hear them. And they have cold bodies tempered with venom. No one can sense their approach at night. Only after they're there do they let their presence be known, stretch out, and then strike, with an out-and-out deadly tenacity. Carlotta shaking her head. She thought again about snakes. In the fear of fatigue, one must deal with sleep. You have to keep in mind that at night, after a night of such terror, new stories will emerge to tell that all of us were in the drainpipe. You, me, the *pioneiro,* the funeral procession to Catete cemetery, the cadavers, pulled there with ropes and stacked in common graves, the health service comrade who happened on a scalp and then displays a photograph they took later of the skull with teeth still gnashing from the final quest for life in the struggle, the skeletal corpses with mottoes stamped on bony mouths where on anonymous roads, because they were abandoned, could mothers never say their sons had been heroes? The girlfriends, weddings put off to after independence only to become widows before their time, brought the news from Cunene two weeks after: "When I get out of this hole I'm heading for Vila Alice to ask comrade Lúcio Lara to let my man come home from the Eastern Front. We'll get married at the *Delegação.* A real MPLA wedding. Then we're going to strut, him in his uniform, all through the Baixa, with the baby too. I wonder if it's a boy or a girl? It's got to be a boy. It's a *pioneiro,* a FAPLA. But even if it's a girl, she'll be a FAPLA." Carlotta rubbing her eyes. She shakes her head. It's important not to fall asleep. Time has passed, a lot of time, in the pipe a fresh breeze and the *pioneiro* has his eyes half-closed in a vigilant sleep in Angolan time: eyes, perhaps, closed, but thoughts wide awake.

That one hit close! Carlotta started, tearing herself away from the dreamlike mental process by means of which she had withstood the passing of the time. Dawn was finally beginning to break. The light prefigured the sun. The *pioneiro* rubbed his eyes with no hint of impatience and then, when he heard a second explosion, leaned his head forward to be able to hear more clearly.

After the fourth explosion, a sudden burst of weapon volleys resounded through the pipe. Automatic weapon fire came from close by and the *pioneiro*'s radiant smile contrasted with the restlessness of a now fully awake Carlotta.

"Is it them?" she asked.

"The mortar is ours. The other guys are fighting back with random fire."

The firefight went on, and after every shell-burst came the wild machine-gun return. Then came two explosions different from the others.

"Whose is that?"

"Our comrades are closing in now. That sound is our bazooka firing," said the *pioneiro*, his face evidencing a new joy.

And then the machine guns repeated their prolonged song, which in turn was interrupted by another burst of fire. Carlotta was also trying eagerly to distinguish among the sounds, until there was a pause in the exchange for a few moments and the boy motioned for them to crawl up closer to the pipe's opening.

"We can hear better," and, saying that, he moved a few more steps toward the opening. Carlotta followed suit. The two located themselves along the same side, as if they were lining up, with the *pioneiro* in front.

A volley reverberated, and single shots as well. The sound wholly distinct from the ones before: hollower, less metallic.

"That's ours," stammered the *pioneiro*, his left hand in the air and his eyes riveted on the opening that led out of their hiding place.

There was another repetition of the disorderly shooting in response.

They were just a short distance from the outside, and the *pioneiro*'s eyes commanded a few meters of the steepest of the ground sloping down to the pipe's entrance. Carlotta could feel the morning humidity in her nostrils and could clearly see her companion, his slingshot rifle, the big boots with no heels and piled-up patches on the toes. It was practically day. But she didn't dare peek out for even a second, and even though she could see without being seen, she lacked the courage to look out on the space controlled by the puppet forces, for they could appear at any moment. She nourished the conviction that her greatest guarantee of getting out of here alive was to wait in this hiding place, because if the ELNA discovered them the child's weapon would be useless. By contrast, the *pioneiro,* in his interest in investigating this turn in the battle with his eyes and his ears, was completely transfixed, his enthusiasm intensifying steadily as the shooting and explosions grew more and more intense.

"The bazookas are starting to zero in. It's a rout!"

The smell of gunpowder reached Carlotta's nose. A smell with which she had become very familiar since the war in Luanda had begun and which never ceased to inspire fear in her. A smell that grew and grew like the noise of pounding fire and shell explosions coming from outside. The boy was radiant, assigning authorship to the various occurrences: "that's ours," "that's theirs," "that's ours," "that's theirs," Carlotta remaining unable to pull herself away from that idea existing somewhere between hopefulness and dejection.

If they're going to find us here it would be better if the *pioneiro* had hidden his weapon back there in the pipe's recesses and taken off his cap and boots and pants, because sometimes when MPLA people are stopped at a FNLA checkpoint they can talk their way out of it by saying things like "my brother" and taking advantage of the prevailing confusion, being sure that their MPLA identification card is well hidden, rolled up tight like a raffle ticket and pressed between body and garment. Some have even chewed up and swallowed cards while waiting their turn to pass through FNLA security. There have been lines of hos-

pital vehicles bearing comrades who had come under artillery fire, a comrade lying on the backseat at times only to
die after clearing security so that it wasn't even worth the
interrogation, questions like who is who? who isn't who?
let me see your papers, why the hospital? where was he
wounded? whose car is it? the dead man's papers? his fa-
ther's name? where did he work? what kind of work? why
so much hatred? even people attempting to save a life and
seeing their own lives hanging by a thread the "People's
House" huh? (what "people"?) everybody knows about
the electric chairs, the gallows, fingernails torn out with
pliers, hair to be force-fed to the dying whose death comes
slowly, and their tormentors swilling whiskey, beer, the
prisoner no longer caring about his pain but seeing his own
blood little by little, so close to that so beautiful time close
to independence with the *tuga* forces favoring the FNLA,
we have heard how the puppets bring arms in across the
Zaire border to kill our people the Portuguese forces look
the other way pretending not to see or just let it happen
and we are surrounded only by sea can arms reach us, but
when ships come in with arms for the people the High
Commissioner declares neutrality and has the cargo confis-
cated, and at the same time the puppets are bringing in
more and more arms across the border and being permitted
by the *tugas*.
    That's theirs
    that's ours
    ours
    ours
    theirs
    The *pioneiro* is also enthralled by the victory if they
are right here and have occupied the area how can we get
out any time soon if they are barricaded in the building and
have a full view in front so that whoever attempts to move
on them will be an open target?

Carlotta covering her eyes with her hands again, her womb convulsing, the child inside and tears, sobs, with no regard for the silence, which in any case had been more than destroyed by the incessant noise of the war, the odor of gunpowder, the youngster engrossed in the reckoning of the fire "ours theirs ours," leaning farther and farther toward the pipe's opening.

The young woman took her hands down from her face. It seemed as if the explosion had been right where they were, chunks of earth flying about, throwing grains of sand down into the pipe. She took courage. She moved to the *pioneiro*'s side, knees on the floor, hands over her belly, head pulled down into her shoulders, her eyes, too, peering out, space visible, little, just a few meters beyond the swale that led down to the pipe. But she was absorbed in the sensation of catching a glimpse of full light. It was day! She had conquered the night!

The big explosion nearby Carlotta closes her eyes opens her eyes in a face peppered with little chunks of earth—My God! It fell right here!—the *pioneiro* alert.

"Ours," spitting saliva laced with mud.

For Carlotta the "ours theirs ours" was no longer of importance. Clearly things were rapidly worsening again and she wanted to get out and the heat of hatred began to boil in her veins, the desire to possess a powerful weapon, open up a withering fire on the building, capture the puppet troops' arms, and then run about shouting in celebration.

"Ours. Ours. Ours. They're really taking a beating now."

"It's ours!" Carlotta responded, clapping her hands together.

And she took renewed confidence in the *pioneiro*.

"Look. Single shots. Ours. They're getting to the building," and he patted the young woman on the back.

Now the volleys began to alternate with single shots. The shell hits stopped, and the *pioneiro* stretched out, his belly on the ground, to try to see farther. Then two explosions resounded. The youngster uttered no comment, and when some outbursts of fire resounded with no reply he pulled himself up on his haunches and unrestrainedly shouted, "Now the fire's only ours. Now it's only ours. Ours!" Carlotta could not react, as though ecstatic, her eyes fixed on the area outside the pipe.

Silence came. She and the *pioneiro* exchanged glances, and suddenly they began to hear the noise of people running. The boy, without uttering a word, immediately pointed with his finger. Carlotta trembled. They could just see legs, up to the knee. There were black boots, green pants, and they were moving as fast as they could from right to left. They were the puppet soldiers. Right there above them, at the top of the incline leading down to the drainpipe. They were the lackeys! Carlotta bit her lip, clenched her fists, and when the sinister parade had passed, looked over at the *pioneiro*.

"Yes, comrade, that was them," said the youngster, understanding the unuttered question.

Then an avalanche of automatic weapon fire broke out, and, in an instinctive reaction, Carlotta threw her arms around the youngster.

"It's ours. All the fire is ours. They're running away." And he stomped on the ground with his boots as though rehearsing a victory march.

The firing stopped. And the distant rumble of motors could be heard. The young woman's eyes on the eyes of the *pioneiro* to see if he could tell whose vehicles those were that were coming closer and closer. The *pioneiro*'s eyes on Carlotta's eyes, but he did not speak, for the first time manifesting puzzlement upon his countenance. Carlotta still with the image of the boots passing so close to her, her heart wildly beating. Now, with the firing died away, everything was very distinct, the motors closer and closer, parking in the environs of the UNTA building, one vehicle speeding up, a solitary outburst of fire, and Carlotta didn't even have time to cry out; she tried to raise her hands and put them over her mouth, but halfway there they ran into the dog as it came back in, eyes wide, tongue hanging out, with a yelping that made its tail move back and forth.

"Bazooka," the boy shouted in greeting. "I'm going out to do reconnaissance." And in a flash, his slingshot rifle in front of him at the ready, he slid through the opening and out of the drain.

Carlotta heard yet another volley, secured her belly with her hands, stared at the figure of the *pioneiro* halfway up the incline, turning around to shout, "The gunfire is ours! Come on out, comrade!"

The young woman took in the group of combatants with an eager look: some in khaki uniforms, others in camouflage, and some in street clothes.

She was bewildered. Then she started to run, bounding toward a blue station wagon, because bursts of fire were still to be heard, albeit now in the distance.

"They're on the run," said one FAPLA.

The vehicle took off with a jerk, and Carlotta saw a jeep start up, too, with *pioneiros* clinging to it all over, one of them raising high, as a victory sign, his slingshot rifle.

The dog was racing after the vehicle.

The *maximbombo* was completely packed. People talking to people even when they didn't know them. Talking loud. Laughing, clapping their hands in joyous rhythm.

"There's no room for any more," they shouted from the rear. "Unless it's a lackey and we can have a people's court in here."

That joke brought a laugh from all the passengers. This was a holiday. Like all the others on which the people came together in victory, forgetting the sacrifices and suffering of the war that Luanda was undergoing in this year nineteen hundred and seventy-five.

"Ready, comrade driver."

The *maximbombo* started to move. It was weighted down, with people hanging on the rear door at the sloping right side, the mudguard almost dragging on the pavement.

"Take this seat, comrade."

Carlotta thanked the man for his considerateness, and, teetering with the bumps, holding on to her newborn child, she sat down in the seat that had been vacated for her.

People packed all along the streets, talking away at the corners, and, if a car came by with FAPLAs in it, arms were raised in the air effusively in the victory V, the soldiers answering back by holding their weapons on high. The euphoria was total. People running from one place to another, street to street, neighborhood to neighborhood, on the hunt for one more morsel of news.

"The FNLA is done for." That's what was on the joyful lips of public Luanda. Nevertheless, in the people's eyes there could be read a determination to discover, wherever they were in the city, those lackeys who were disoriented and dispersed.

The bus stopped. Passengers got off and others got on, all of them in a commotion.

"They caught three, weapons and all," someone announced.

"Where?" others immediately asked.

"They were clearing out of the Saneamento and some comrades over near Praia do Bispo grabbed them. I saw it all."

"Don't go yet, comrade," came a shout from outside. The driver did as he was asked. Carlotta looked out the window: the group was armed with brushes and cans of paint. Inside the *maximbombo*, everything in an uproar as the latest war news was being told and heard.

"Look here, people! You should see what happened on Avenida Brasil! They really took a beating. I can't believe there's anyone left to report back to Mobutu."

"Or to Kissinger," added a young man.

"Who's that?"

"He's the American. Look here. It's reactionary not to read the newspapers. Or at least listen to the radio."

"OK, OK. But who told you that I'm not illiterate, comrade? By the way, it just so happens that I'm not."

"Attention, comrades." And everyone turned to listen. Have you heard the news? I just came through Vila Alice and they were saying that the FNLA is fleeing to São Pedro da Barra fort."

"Let 'em go. There we can just pick them off."

"You can go now, comrade," shouted a young man from outside, his arm stretched out and a paintbrush in his hand.

The *maximbombo* started into motion again, bearing in dripping letters of yellow paint: "MPLA THE VICTORY IS CERTAIN."

"This mania for painting the *maximbombos*, even the houses are all marked up."

"Let them paint. We'll get lackeys to clean it all up."

Carlotta, her eyes glued to the bus window, savored this bit of graffiti painted on a building wall: "Revolution is like a bicycle: if it stops, it falls over."

"Now a body can show her MPLA card and dress in an OMA uniform without fear."

The woman was standing on tiptoe, holding high between the outstretched fingers of a raised hand, for everyone to see, the militant's identification card she had pulled out from her bosom.

"Imagine! Not too long ago I even had to bury this card when they were carrying out searches in my neighborhood. Now I can show it for everyone to see. Are there any FNLA supporters here? If there are, just look at this. I bet there are some lackeys here! They're not crowing today, are they? They've lost their voices."

The bus arrived at Mutamba station. Huge throngs of people under the shelters at the several bus stops, in the same state of agitation as was exuded throughout the city. Carlotta could tell, through the window, what one of the major topics of conversation was. The FNLA were beginning to concentrate in the Saneamento neighborhood, near the puppet ministers' homes. Some were going around in street clothes with their weapons hidden in bundled cloth or newspaper. Others were going into the government area completely armed and equipped. The *tuga* troops at the checkpoints were looking the other way.

"The FNLA has summoned all the people from the North to the Palace, and the UNITA has summoned all the people from the South."

"Have you gone to see for sure, comrade?" asked another male voice.

"To Sambizanga. This is what they're saying: everybody from the North and the South should go to the Palace right away, raise a lot of commotion requesting transportation home because here in Luanda the communists are going to kill everyone from the North and from the South."

"He's telling the truth. They're trying to deceive the people by appealing to tribalism. The worst thing is that the BJR is in the Palace area in disguise. This is going to take a while."

"We have to mobilize action groups to round up every one of those bums."

The *maximbombo* had now finished letting off and taking on passengers. It was now fuller than before, the hot motor shrieking with fatigue. As they went through the first intersection, Carlotta held the baby under its arms and stuck her head out of the bus window.

"*Pioneiro!* Oh, comrade *pioneiro!*" She started in with an instinctive movement to get up and ask the driver to stop. Too late. The corner had been left behind.

"That was him; it clearly was," Carlotta said to herself, overcome with emotion.

Three months had passed. Three months of sporadic days during which the panic of weapons fire, of rapes, of massacres, was absent. Three months in which Carlotta had recounted to almost all her friends and acquaintances the adventure of the drainpipe, passionately extolling the *pioneiro*'s heroism. Three months spent scrutinizing all the boys she came across in her great desire to find the mysterious *pioneiro*. Now Carlotta bore in her arms the son who, still in the womb, had shared that night of resistance inside the pipe. "That was him, it *was*," she kept thinking, now oblivious to the bustle on the streets through which the overloaded bus was traveling, complete with the wet paint on its side running and making the letters larger and larger.

"It *was* him, it *was*." After three long months, Carlotta had succeeded in finding the *pioneiro* again. "It *was* him." The *pioneiro* with the slingshot rifle who peered through the night and catalogued the war—"that's ours, theirs, ours, ours"—with an unassailable optimism flashing in the moonlit glow of his eyes. The *pioneiro* who belonged to the Kwenha squadron and was friends with a dog named Bazooka.

The *maximbombo* climbed up to Vila Alice. Carlotta got off. The groups dispersed at the COL, across from the *Delegação* and the SAM. Cars were coming and going, still hot from the recent fray. And everyone evidenced hunger in his or her eyes for a piece of news to receive or to give out.

She climbed the stairs. She went into the Department of Information and Publicity and burst out: "Mother, I saw the *pioneiro*."

"Where, my child?"

"Near the Mutamba station. From inside the bus. I called and called, but he didn't hear me."

"What *pioneiro*?" Comrade Osvaldo asked in a distracted voice.

"This obsession of yours to find <u>the</u> *pioneiro*. There are so many *pioneiros*. You have a *pioneiro* in your own arms right now. Angola is a country of *pioneiros*, and that's why the lackeys can't win. Is it true about your son's name?"

"I'm going to name him after the *pioneiro* who saved me from the FNLA."

"And because of all the confusion you didn't even ask him what his name was."

"I'm going to find out."

"Oh, this MPLA . . . " And directing his gaze far out beyond the balcony of the building: "It's going to be one hell of a job to get that cabal out of São Pedro da Barra."

You could walk through the streets of Luanda at night now, and it was a joy to see the people along Avenida Brasil, looking at the blackened, pockmarked building. In some neighborhoods, the *pioneiros* were taking the old puppet bases by storm and then intoning their revolutionary songs, playing the part of the lackeys in pantomime, and practicing their famed marching style, with an eye to the upcoming independence parade.

Luanda was virtually free of the puppets, but the war itself had not yet ended. In Vila Alice, Carlotta listened to and participated in all the discussions. Foodstuffs became scarce. The exodus to the North and to the South instigated by the puppets created an enormous tension in the people, a fear for the immediate future.

"You can see it now," Comrade Osvaldo pontificated. "The war is going to spread throughout the whole country. In the North, the Zaireens are coming in and going back across the border at will and massacring entire populations. Down below, the South Africans. And the Portuguese troops collaborating in the whole business. And didn't the UNITA and FNLA ministers leave the city with all the contents of the houses of state and everything but the walls from the Palace chambers? And the *tuga* troops going along with that farce. Shit on that kind of 'active neutrality'! They're using tribalism to try to balkanize the country," he concluded in an angry tone. He folded the newspaper he had been holding and flung it on top of a desk. He hadn't even laid an eye on it.

It was eleven o'clock at night. Carlotta came in with an aluminum coffee pot, steam rising out of it. The comrades in the office, enticed by the coffee smell, began picking up their plastic cups and preparing for the customary break. *Delegação* nights where, when drowsiness began to settle in, the militants would lie down in shifts on the floor just to stretch their bodies for a few moments.

Carlotta sat at one of the empty desks. She picked up the newspaper. On the first page, left-hand side, an extensive article on the situation at the port of Luanda. The interminable line of vehicles that the "returnees" were sending back to Portugal. The crates. And the writer spent a great deal of time on the so-called love that the settlers said they had for Angola, as they left with all the speed they could muster, their only concern being to take with them all the goods and products they could, stained with the sweat of the Angolan people, and, what is even more, contraband in diamonds, gold, marijuana, hard currency, and even piles of colonial bank notes. The writer concluded: "Yesterday, in an ironmonger's in the downtown, a Portuguese citizen asked to see the firm's manager and, displaying a huge wad of bank notes, said: 'I want you to crate three hundred *contos'* worth of merchandise for me. Price is no object.' " The article was illustrated with a picture of crates at the port, with the caption "Down with exploitation by the crateload!"

Then Carlotta read in the middle of the page the headline, in large letters, "The people's vigilance reveals yet another puppet crime." She devoured the first lines of the story. The FNLA had been using volunteer fire vehicles to transport weapons. One fireman had confessed that the interior minister had been the brains behind the scheme and that he had forced some of the members of the fire department to carry it out. The fireman revealed the existence of a huge cache of arms and munitions buried at the department's yard. Carlotta was enthralled to read: "At the bottom of the investigations leading to the revelation of this additional instance of outrageous tactics employed by the imperialist lackeys was the vigilance of our *pioneiros.*" She turned the page to continue reading the article and saw a picture with the caption "MPLA *pioneiros* actively participate in the anti-imperialist struggle."

There were eight of them. Four lined up two and two, with another rank of three. In profile. At their head, a commander with a checkered shirt. And, on the left side in the last rank, "It was him!" His face was partly covered, but "It was him," you could tell by his stature, by his boots.

128

"Mama! I *am* going to find the *pioneiro*. The newspaper has a photograph of him. Look!"

Comrade Stella gently placed in the basket the grandson she had been holding and walked over, with curiosity, to her daughter's side.

"Which one?"

"That one there."

"You can hardly see his face."

"I know. But I recognize him. And this is his commander, Kwenha. I'm going down to the newspaper tomorrow."

The nights were different in Vila Alice. Tracers no longer darted across the sky between Avenida Brasil and João de Almeida Street with their messages of death, and the air could be breathed hot but calm, tempered for new times.

"Shell explosions, Comrade Osvaldo?" asked Comrade Stella without betraying the slightest apprehension. "Far away."

"Yes. It's the young folks shooting at the fort. That could lead to problems. There is always the danger that we'll hit the oil refinery. The fire from that could level the whole city."

It was past one o'clock. Carlotta went down the stairs. Tonight there was enough coffee for the soldiers who, as a precaution, still patrolled the nearby blocks. And she was going to portion it out.

You could walk without fear now, all the way to Avenida Brasil.

"Good morning, comrade. I wish to speak to the comrade director."

"I don't know if he is in. Let's go see."

"Yes, comrade. What a mess you have here."

"It was because of the bomb," observed the office worker, gesturing toward the piles of rubble, from which a few rooms had been spared, for out from the heaps of fragmented concrete, brick, wood beams, paper, and tile came the noise of machines running.

"Be careful here," the employee advised.

Carlotta stepped out softly onto the wood planking, looking down onto the ground floor below.

"This was an FNLA newspaper before, wasn't it, comrade?"

"Yes it was. But it's ours now. We took it over right after the explosion."

"And the old director?"

"They say he fled to South Africa. You wouldn't believe what was going on in here. ELNA soldiers, comrades who were missing. You can't imagine what all. But our action group won out."

"Underground, huh?"

"Yes, comrade. But also they needed us. The only typesetters available were MPLA. Without our people everything would have ground to a halt."

Carlotta breathed in the smell of ink and paper at this headquarters of a newspaper that had for months distributed all the FNLA propaganda, publishing blown-up photos of the puppet ministers' hideous faces mouthing speeches that were nothing more than threats against "people power."

"It looks like he *is* available," said the office worker.

Carlotta made her way through a jumble of editing desks.

"Good morning, Comrade Director."

"Good morning. How may I help you?"

"I have come about a *pioneiro* in the picture you published yesterday. I need to find him."

"But why, comrade?" He already had a copy of the previous day's newspaper open to page two.

Carlotta wanted to tell the whole, long story, the UNTA building, the shooting, the bombardment. But she just timidly summed up: "I spent an entire night under fire with him and then never saw him again. I don't even know his name."

The director betrayed an air of exasperation and, with a jerk, pushed his head forward on his neck.

"First of all, I can't even say with certainty that those were the actual *pioneiros* who discovered the weapons that Kabangu had buried in the firemen's yard. In such circumstances we frequently use an available photograph, just for illustration, you understand. Or it might have been that our photographer was unable to get to the scene, or by the time he did the *pioneiros* had already gone. What's more, in the last little while almost all our photographic material has come from the ministry. But we can find out." And, turning to one of the editors: "Is Comrade Guilherme here?"

"No. He's out on assignment," answered the editor, without pausing in his typewriting.

"See? We're hard at work here. In the second place, we *are* at war. At this very moment some of our comrades are covering the fighting at the fronts. For all practical purposes, we are down to four editors around here. Therefore we cannot give much time to incidental problems. And, just so you know, we are not allowed to publish personals that haven't been cleared by the ministry. We are at war, and information is like a FAPLA soldier: a weapon. Even in radio programming only emergency matters are broadcast. Forgive me, I am sorry . . . but as a militant I must criticize you severely."

Carlotta didn't even say good-bye. She walked hurriedly down the hallway, went out through the wooden door, and descended the stairs four at a time.

She headed toward the Ministry of Information. But why hadn't she explained that she owed her life to that *pioneiro?* That she was with him for an entire night inside the drainpipe? No. She would go into the ministry and speak up about it.

Emboldened in her determination, she kept resolutely walking with the intent of getting inside the Palace. She had to find that *pioneiro.* The *pioneiro* who kept count of the shell hits and the shots and was ever confident of victory. The *pioneiro* armed with a little slingshot rifle, ready to blast the first lackey to try to enter their hiding place.

She reached Mutamba Square. Line after line of people waiting for the *maximbombos.* And once again the image that was etched on her mind: she had seen them go by, on that very corner. In the picture in the newspaper they appeared in a formation with two ranks of two and another of three. The one with the checkered shirt was the commander. Her *pioneiro* was on the left end of the rank of three and his face was hard to make out. But it *was* him, the *pioneiro* who was friends with a dog named Bazooka. *That's ours that's theirs that's ours.* Carlotta broke into a run, startling some bystanders.

Irritatingly, at the door of the Palace the guard of *tuga* marines subjected her to a search. They opened and closed her bag with a perfunctory automatism, almost not looking at its contents.

Bedlam reigned in the office of public information services: some people typing, others taking telephone calls, the doors repeatedly opening and closing as employees passed through in the exchange of documents. But no one spoke, and Carlotta could see the strain of overwork on the employees' faces.

"How may I help you, comrade?"

She gave a long look over the employee's face, her frantic air, glasses suspended from a metal chain hanging around her neck.

"I am an MPLA militant, and . . . "

"Yes, comrade. So am I. But let's get straight down to business. What can I do?"

"I spent a night hiding inside a drainpipe. Under fire. Next to the UNTA building. There was a *pioneiro* who saved my life. I don't know his name. I passed him the other day but I was inside a *maximbombo* and couldn't get out to reach him. He's in the Kwenha squadron. Yesterday a picture of him appeared in the *Journal of Angola*. They may have been the squadron that discovered the firemen's weapons. I've gone to the newspaper, to no avail. They say that perhaps the picture came from here. And I want that *pioneiro* who . . . "

"Really, comrade!" the employee cut in, standing up in a fury. A militant, ha! If you had come to try to find a missing relative, maybe. But a *pioneiro?* Hundreds of photographs pass through our hands in here. And 'Kwenha squadron'? There are many, many *pioneiro* squadrons with that name. There are many, many *pioneiros*. Really! You're going to have to engage in some self-criticism. Listen to the radio program 'Last Word about the Situation' when it comes on today. It was confirmed less than an hour ago. The UNITA has taken Huambo. They're killing all the militants there and all the Movement sympathizers. The comrades at the Center for Revolutionary Instruction were massacred, we know that Comrade Muteka was killed and mutilated, Comrades Kapango and Machado were in the process of escaping but the *tuga* troops allowed the puppets to take them after they were in the airplane. And you interrupt our work with some story about a *pioneiro?* There are many, many stories about *pioneiros*. We have lost Huambo! We have lost Huambo!"

"I am sorry, comrade."

She ran out of the building, and, once outside, broke into nervous sobbing. Huambo was in UNITA hands! Yes, it was incorrect of her to bother the ministry about the *pioneiro* on this day, with all the workers in a panic. The comrade with the glasses hanging from the chain was right. There *were* many *pioneiros*. And any number of Kwenha squadrons. But that *pioneiro* was different. He had stayed with her inside the drainpipe. Brave. A hero. The ministry comrade was right. But so was she; the unfortunate coincidence of this disastrous day, Huambo fallen to the puppets, wasn't her fault. Maybe the comrades in Vila Alice hadn't heard the news yet, since it had been confirmed so recently. She had to hurry to tell her mother and Comrade Osvaldo.

Every firearm in Luanda was discharged into the ancient sky. Carlotta, in a small space opened up by a cordon of FAPLAs, her eyes picking out the speaker's platform, then the flagpole, the *pioneiro,* this year's fourth of February hero, the voices of the chorus from the "Jota"* singing the new anthem reached her ears, with her taking in each word avidly, eyes following the slow rise of the flag, which also was new, and the second time the "Jota" sang the refrain she immediately memorized it:

> *Onward Angola,*
>
> *Revolution,*
>
> *For the Power of the People*
>
> *United Country, Freedom*
>
> *One United People, One United Nation.*

---

* *Jota* is the Portuguese word for the letter *j*. Here it refers to "MPLA Youth," in Portuguese, *Juventude do MPLA,* a youth choir.

The chorus finished its rendition of the anthem the shouting rose in competition with the salvo of gunfire spotlights like a flashbulb further illuminated the area around the flagpole the flag in Carlotta's eyes.

"It's almost the same as the MPLA flag. Hooray!" arms raised, hands avidly reaching for the symbols—machete, gear wheel, and star—all against the red-and-black background of the mother flag on fatherland First of May Square teeming with people, that human mass transmuting the suffering of war into the joy of independence.

> *"In the name of the Angolan People,*
>
> *the Central Committee of the Popular*
>
> *Movement for the Liberation of*
>
> *Angola (MPLA) solemnly proclaims,*
>
> *before Africa and the World, the*
>
> *Independence of Angola."*

Carlotta on First of May Square, her thoughts going back to the pipe. The drainpipe. Carlotta's eyes on the *pioneiro*'s eyes the little slingshot rifle the hat the incongruous boots FNLA volleys that's theirs ours theirs ours it was dark in the pipe the lizards then it was hard to get through the night but light came and in the Mutamba she ran across the *pioneiro* who was in the picture the whole squadron. Eight of them. Four by twos and three together. The commander with the checkered shirt. Today is Independence Day—today, today eleventh of November 1975 it has been proclaimed Comrade President said that the Central Committee decided the people decided and inside Carlotta the conviction the *pioneiro* is going to be found is

reborn running with him to the UNTA building the two going down into the drain saying the MPLA order words
without fear. She and the *pioneiro* who was friends with a
dog named Bazooka independence day the puppets with
mercenaries desperately trying to penetrate beyond the
Caxito line.

All imperialist lackeys if it's an armored car I'll blow
the operator up armor can't run without humans a comrade said at a rally that it's the man who makes the machine if it's a ship like a battleship then the fisherfolk who
are organized and are for the MPLA and if enemy boats
come we'll sink them and if it's an airplane just let it fly
low and I'll shoot it down a comrade told me he shot down
a 'copter in the first war.

If it's armor I'll blow up the operator if it's a ship I'll
sink it if it's an airplane I'll shoot it down.

The people behind want to see the festivities too it's
for everyone comrade! the FAPLA cordon the OPA the
"Jota" the OMA helping with crowd control impossible
today, the eleventh of November, five hundred years of cordons today the people want to see Comrade Neto up close
up closer much closer than the other times the FAPLA cordon still closing off the OPA the "Jota" the OMA in the
control of the joy and Carlotta from the front from the
sides being jostled without protesting even pressing against
the rope looking out at the open expanse of the street another cordon on the other side with police comrades and
pioneiros the checkered shirt it's him! it's him! the order
words, shots in the air, loudspeakers "now comrades we're
all going to the Palace, the people's Palace" it wasn't on the
program for the cordons to collapse before the onrushing
crowd the checkered shirt in Carlotta's eyes everyone filling the street all the people pushing to try to be first to get
to the Palace for the first time the People's intoning:

"On the morning of February Fourth

the heroes threw off the shackles"

The OMA singing marching with difficulty in the crush of the crowd the avenue overflowing Carlotta stuck in place the checkered shirt moving away "Pardon me please let me through comrade" the jam at the intersection the military hospital a more open space and she resolved not to lose sight of the commander's shirt "Kwenha they called him" with her sharp eyes on the frantic march *pioneiros* preparing to march too. Brand-new OPA shirts. But that wasn't them. Then a huge OMA formation, now in the "sacred family" a FAPLA fired a volley resonating close in Carlotta's ears as she no longer makes out the checkered shirt with certainty they were going on forward to be the first to the Palace "let me through comrade" and from the windows verandas and yards pour even those less demonstrative people to celebrate and watch people pass by and in Maianga Square Carlotta bumps into a portable tape recorder from which a recording of the national anthem could be heard "pardon me comrade where did you get it?" "I recorded it a few minutes ago in the square" "it's so beautiful I couldn't stand it."

And before her the human wave growing denser and denser the multitude funneling itself along the road to the Palace and even so some were frustrated, like Carlotta, who wasn't even able to get into the Palace Square with the anthem's refrain in her head the *pioneiro* must be there but she only heard the words of a speech and the multitude all in one voice in "the struggle goes on" and "victory is certain" where the squadron and the heroic *pioneiro* of the drainpipe might be now is impossible to tell. To discover. Her. Carlotta. Still the shots, darkness the target. The people dispersing back into the city in the neighborhoods independence celebration continuing on. Carlotta lights cigarettes, the next one on the last. Quick steps taken in no particular direction. Little importance in the pockmarked gray house. She stopped for a short time. Contemplative. Not a sound from inside the building. On top, the MPLA flag. The building from which they would launch tracers and bursts from the heavy machine gun that the *pioneiro* could single out. It had also been the control center. She looked behind, up the long street, the whole, long way, Avenida Brasil, and had the sensation that the posts, the lights, the walls held within them a multitude of stories to be told, of numbers of people assassinated, stories of the anonymous popular resistance. Sometimes carried out just with hands. Or teeth. Or with the audacity to answer the first act of aggression with the MPLA order words. What could be left inside? A mixture of fear and nausea ran through her body. She had been on her feet in First of May Square starting two hours before the ceremony began. Then all that distance to the area of the Palace. She now had a defined objective. Nevertheless, she walked, absorbed in the distraction of her thoughts' wandering through the immediate past. Tracers. Mortar rounds. Ambulances racing at high speeds. And everything disconnected related only by the fatigue, the will not to succumb to sleep, to just walk through time prolonging the night, and Carlotta saw herself lifting her feet vigorously, stretching out her arms, beating her breast with one fist, then with the other, her stride unmatchable. Like in the OPA parades. The *pioneiro* beside her. With the little slingshot rifle, the oversized, incongruous boots almost kicking the stars on the vault of the sky.

She reached the UNTA building. Exhausted. Breathing in through her mouth the hot breath that ran through the air. She went to the front door. A soldier sitting on the steps, softly whistling.

"Good evening, comrade. Doing sentry duty?"

"Yes, comrade," and, getting to his feet, "do you happen to have a cigarette?"

And he lit the cigarette avidly on Carlotta's; he turned his head in the direction of a new echo of firing.

"Are you coming from the independence celebration?"

"Yes, comrade. How long have you been on duty here?"

"I got here this afternoon. Today. In Caxito. I counted twenty-seven shell hits. The puppets failed to get into Luanda, though. Believe me, they're never going to wet their feet on this beach again." He smoked the cigarette behind a shell made with his hands, the fingers held together to hide the ember.

"And the celebration? They told me this afternoon that there's a national anthem."

"Yes, comrade."

"What's it like?"

"I only know the part that they repeat once. There are two other parts. The little bit I know goes like this," and she sang through the refrain.

The soldier was delighted, and when Carlotta finished singing the refrain for the third time, he took another long drag on the cigarette and wanted to know:

"Is the MPLA flag going to keep being the flag?"

"No, comrade."

"What's the new one like," he wondered, evidencing his concern and disappointment.

"It's almost the same. Red and black like the Movement flag. And it also has the yellow star along with the machete and something that looks like half a wagon wheel. But more beautiful than any other flag in the whole world, comrade."

"But then it really is the same!"

"Yes, comrade. And there was a huge amount of firing in First of May Square. Today every FAPLA in Luanda has probably fired a shot into the air. You too, I'll bet."

"Not a one. Discipline is discipline," he concluded, grabbing his weapon by the clip.

The soldier drew the cigarette down to the filter and tossed the butt onto the ground, stepping on it. He looked at Carlotta with inquisitorial curiosity. And she asked:

"The building is ruined on the inside, isn't it? They tore everything apart, didn't they?"

"Pretty much. But why have you come here at this late hour of the night to ask that?"

"I worked at the UNTA. In this building. The day the FNLA shelled and invaded the installation I was inside and a *pioneiro* saved me. Then the two of us hid down in that pipe over there. Our comrades didn't get here to drive them out until early morning. Me. And the *pioneiro*."

She sat down on the steps and began telling the story, past and present, slowly. Herself with the *pioneiro*. Details of the boy's "theirs ours" reading the battle. The victory over the puppets witnessed from within the pipe. The unburdening that Carlotta had long desired as she told the story about herself and the *pioneiro*. And so everything was told in minute detail, from the first bombardment of the building, the sense of danger, Comrade Cook's screams told for the first time. Carlotta hadn't even gone through it all like this, detail after detail, for her mother. Shooting bazookas complete with gestures, filling her cheeks to reproduce the sound of explosions, vomiting up a volley tu-tu-tu-tum, machine gun in her hands—him saying that it was high fire single shots ours people can't be wasting munitions ta-ta-ta-ta they're going to take a fierce beating the pipe was very dark the lizards licked my hair they weren't lizards because I shook my head the *pioneiro* in front of me laughing I was eight months pregnant but wait a bit on the story of the dog I don't know if I've said that it was called the Kwenha squadron I'll explain in a minute how they did their formation the commander wears a black-and-white checkered shirt it looks like the flag the *tugas* used when they held car races here; there came the picture in the newspaper of four formed two and two and three in one rank because with their commander in front they don't come out in an even formation. The dog's name is Bazooka, oh, and that drain is base number five of the Kwenha squadron and the dog frightened me I thought he was an FNLA when he came in I screamed in the end he was the one that came to inform us that the comrades had eliminated the danger. I've already told about the puppet legs we saw, my God! but let me tell you how the *pioneiro* saved me up above here in the office huddling behind the curtains.

Carlotta lost in the narrative, giving every detail of the smell, the heat, the light, all translated into gesture-word-sounds, and the soldier, with his hand in a permanent shell, Carlotta smoking one cigarette after another, listened to what was a story of legendary quality about a *pioneiro* who might never have existed but who was the same as all the other *pioneiros* living and dying every victorious morning in that deadly serious war game of theirs.

And the night, punctuated by the glorious firing, now extended its fatigued arms to the outlines of the morning. Stars fleeing to their daytime repose. Morning sounds were blossoming. Flowers, touched by the wind that had known so many heroes, released the fresh, sweet dew at the earth's mouth. Then when the sun had arisen from the ancient, violated sea of days before, letting down its flowing hair of light and strength, Carlotta paused an instant to contemplate it. It was the first sun under freedom.

"The sun is born. The first day after independence! It seems like a dream, comrade."

The guerrilla sprang to his feet, took two steps forward, pointed his rifle to the vestiges of the moon, and expended his entire clip in one single volley.

"Yes, comrade," he said after blowing the smoke from the barrel.

And this powder smell invading Carlotta's nose seemed to her a perfume.

Part Two

A few minutes before eight o'clock at night. The *Delegação* employees joyfully tick off the countries that have now recognized the People's Republic of Angola. Carlotta with her ears tuned to the radio. Independence had been proclaimed for almost four days now.

She had pulled herself away from her cares and, with the *pioneiro* in mind, had gone to the Department of Information and Publicity. It was the people's radio, and every day on "Angola at War" comrades revealed the many different things that had happened in the war: torture, puppet defeats, grotesque scenes of cannibalism on the part of the ELNA butchers, hasty retreats. And acts of courage by *pioneiro* children.

And Carlotta had been successful. She spoke into a tape recorder for almost four minutes.

As soon as the anthem penetrated her ears, she turned up the sound. The comrade broadcaster read the editorial about the People's Republic of Angola and the anti-imperialist struggle, to motivate the people from Cabinda to Cunene to produce more so that resistance could be more effective. And he ended, "To produce is to resist. The struggle goes on! Victory is certain!"

Then, when he announced the testimonies, Carlotta

glued her ear to the machine. The announcer praised the *pioneiros'* role in the General Popular Resistance.

"Mama," shouted Carlotta. "I'm going to talk now."

"Comrades! Here is another story involving the glorious M-P-L-A *pioneiros.* How did the *pioneiro* find you?"

"I was behind some curtains . . . " And she spoke about the cook's screams, the boots' noise, the furious trip down the stairs, the drainpipe, the mortar rounds. "That *pioneiro* is a hero. He saved my life. His squadron was called the Kwenha squadron."

"If you saw him again, would you recognize him?"

"Yes, comrade. I saw his picture in the *Journal of Angola* when the arms were discovered near the fire station. The commander wears a black-and-white shirt. The *pioneiro* is friends with a dog named Bazooka, and I am very anxious to get into contact with him."

"What you have just heard is an appeal to the comrade *pioneiro* who, in an act of revolutionary valor, saved Comrade Carlotta's life. 'Angola at War' is waiting to hear in your own words as well about the adventure of the drainpipe that ended in another defeat for the imperialist lackeys. Down with the imperialist lackeys!"

"Now I'm really going to find the *pioneiro,*" exulted Carlotta, jumping up from her chair.

And for the rest of the night, while she worked on packages of pennants with the national anthem on the back, Carlotta convinced herself that the *pioneiro* would show up on "Angola at War." Maybe even on tomorrow's program.

Angola had been independent for five days now. Eleven o'clock in the morning. In Vila Alice, people coming and going, hungry for news. A roar of vehicles caught up still in the traffic. Carlotta helping her mother with the typing. Then someone shouted from the door:

"Comrade Osvaldo, some people have just arrived from Caxito."

"Good news, or not?"

"I don't know."

"Yes sir, good news," answered a voice at the end of the line in the hallway. They have captured a mercenary. He's an Englishman."

Carlotta stood up and went over to the balcony to see. There were four FAPLA platoons, faces smudged with dust, uniforms half ripped apart. The people began to surround the soldiers.

Carlotta's eyes blinking. To one side, a *pioneiro* formation. A checkered shirt, black and white.

"Mama. It's him."

"Who?" asked Comrade Osvaldo, running toward the stairs.

"Let's go see the *pioneiro,* my little son." And with her baby in her arms, she also started downstairs, following after her mother and Comrade Osvaldo.

"I'll be damned! They got a mercenary. Now there's big game. I'd like to see him let loose in a *musseque* with a sign on his back," Comrade Osvaldo was saying to himself, in a state of agitation. Just outside the door, speaking to the commander:

"Comrade, where is this mercenary?"

"He was taken into the barracks."

The commander answered calmly, manifesting a certain disdain for the victorious tone in Comrade Osvaldo's voice.

"So how did it go?" inquired Comrade Stella.

With the back of a bandaged hand the commander wiped his mouth, streaked with dirt and saliva. He took off his beret and rubbed his head, his eyes fixed on the ground.

144

"We had to retreat. The battle was against all mercenaries."

"Did you take casualties?"

"Yes. There was a bazooka hit. Three soldiers killed and one boy — one of those kids who have the crazy habit of hiding in our trucks when we go out on night patrol. We left the other comrades there in retreat and came to get reinforcements. But we got at least twenty-one. Confirmed."

Carlotta hearing the commander's words and trying to push through the mass of people who had got there ahead of her and kept her from seeing between the door and the formation. Then, right next to the soldiers, the shoulder of the checkered shirt moved from right to left the Kwenha squadron was passing close Carlotta looked carefully from right to left looking over the *pioneiros* one by one pants shirt hat feet face counting over and over one two three four five six with the commander makes seven.

No *pioneiro* from the drainpipe with light in his eyes like the sun on that first morning. November. Eleventh. The *pioneiro* who catalogued the war "ours theirs ours theirs" had boots that were much too large with patched-up toes, a little slingshot rifle, a dog named Bazooka, and was always convinced that victory is certain if it were armor he'd blow up the operator if it were a ship he'd sink it and if it were a plane he'd shoot it down.

The *pioneiro* who had died five days after independence when the mercenaries persisted in crossing the Caxito front.

And now there were seven in the patrol, formed three and three, for the formation now came out even with the commander out in front.

Five days after independence.

List of Organizations

BJR   An FNLA spy corps. (What the letters refer to is unclear.)

ELNA   Army of Angolan National Liberation (Exército de Libertação Nacional de Angola). The name given to the FNLA military forces.

FAPLA   The People's Armed Forces for the Liberation of Angola (Forças Armadas Populares de Libertação de Angola). The name given to the MPLA military forces.

FNLA   National Front for the Liberation of Angola (Frente Nacional da Libertação de Angola).

MPLA   Popular Movement for the Liberation of Angola (Movimento Popular de Libertação de Angola).

OMA   The MPLA's Angolan Women's Organization (Organização da Mulher Angolana).

OPA	People's Organization of Angola (Organização Popular de Angola). An MPLA building and organization.
UNITA	National Union for the Total Independence of Angola (União Nacional para a Independência Total de Angola).
UNTA	Angolan Workers' Union (União de Trabalhadores Angolanos).
UPA	People's Union of Angola (União Popular de Angola). Eventually became the FNLA.

Manuel Rui, an Angolan, is one of the leading writers of postcolonial Angolan fiction. He has published several works of fiction and poetry, including *Regresso Adiado* (1973), *Sim Camarada!* (1977), *Memória de Mar* (1980), and *Quem me dera ser onda* (1982). None of his works has until now been available in English translation.

Ronald Sousa is professor of comparative literature at the University of Minnesota. He is the author of *The Rediscoverers: Major Figures in the Portuguese Literature of National Regeneration* and the translator of Clarice Lispector's *The Passion according to G.H.* (University of Minnesota Press, 1988)

Gitahi Gititi, who was born in Kenya, is assistant professor of English at the University of Rhode Island at Kingston, where he teaches African, Caribbean, Latin American, and North American literatures. He received his M.A. from the University of Nairobi and his Ph.D. from the University of Minnesota. He has taught literature at Kenyatta University in Nairobi and at Yale University.